KT-196-687

Bristol Library Service

AN 3022966 9

THE PRINCE'S
SECRET BRIDE

THE PRINCE'S SECRET BRIDE

BY

RAYE MORGAN

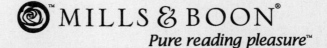

MILLS & BOON®
Pure reading pleasure™

All the characters in this book have no existence
outside the imagination of the author, and have
no relation whatsoever to anyone bearing the same
name or names. They are not even distantly inspired
by any individual known or unknown to the author,
and all the incidents are pure invention.

All Rights Reserved including the right of
reproduction in whole or in part in any form.
This edition is published by arrangement with
Harlequin Enterprises II BV/S.à.r.l. The text of this
publication or any part thereof may not be reproduced
or transmitted in any form or by any means, electronic
or mechanical, including photocopying, recording,
storage in an information retrieval system, or otherwise,
without the written permission of the publisher.

® and TM are trademarks owned and used by the
trademark owner and/or its licensee. Trademarks
marked with ® are registered with the United Kingdom
Patent Office and/or the Office for Harmonisation in
the Internal Market and in other countries.

First published in Great Britain 2008
Large Print edition 2008
Harlequin Mills & Boon Limited,
Eton House, 18-24 Paradise Road,
Richmond, Surrey TW9 1SR

© Helen Conrad 2008

ISBN: 978 0 263 20105 5

Set in Times Roman 16½ on 19 pt.
16-1208-48765

Printed and bound in Great Britain
by CPI Antony Rowe, Chippenham, Wiltshire

To my friend Patty Jackson,
who is going to London to see the Queen!

CHAPTER ONE

PRINCE Nico of the royal House of Montenevada pulled down his cap and turned his collar up, partly against the misting drizzle, but also in order to avoid being recognized. His family had been back in power less than six months and he was already sick of the toll it was taking on his private life. He hadn't spent five years leading a rebellion in the mountains so that he could be treated like a rock star. He'd thought they were fighting for bigger things. Now he wasn't so sure.

The dark streets were pretty much deserted and only dimly lit by flickering street lamps. A lone car went by. Then a cluster of giggling teenagers, late for their curfews. As he started over the Gonglia Bridge, he passed a young woman whose eyes were strangely vacant; she seemed to gaze right through him. Her mass of blond crimped curls was wild around her pretty face, but that seemed to be a style that was popular these days and he didn't think twice about it. That otherworldly look in her eyes stayed with him, though, and when he reached the high point of the bridge's arc, he turned and looked back to see what she was doing.

"Hey!"

What he saw had him running back. The crazy woman was about to jump! In the half a minute since he'd passed her, she'd climbed out on the scaffolding and was leaning over the inky waters that rolled beneath, racing down out of the mountains toward the sea.

"Hold it!" he yelled as he flung himself at her.

She looked up, startled, and tried to avoid him, twisting away so that she was even more danger-ously close to crashing down into the river. He grabbed her roughly. There was no time for niceties. Gripping her upper arm, he sank his other hand into her thick hair and yanked her back onto solid surface. She fell against him and he had just time to take in the soft, round feel of her breast as his palm unintentionally slid over it, before she turned on him like a scalded cat.

"Get away!" she cried, glaring at him and backing away. "Leave me alone!"

He grimaced, annoyed with her, annoyed with anyone who would make such an obvious play for attention as jumping from a bridge. And then her soft blue jacket fell open enough for him to see her body and he realized that she was pregnant. That put a different light on things. He winced, knowing from experience that a pregnancy could change everything—for everyone involved. He looked deeply into her wide dark eyes and saw something that tugged at his sympathies after all.

"I'd be happy to leave you alone," he said, trying to shave any harshness from his comments, "if you think you could refrain from flinging yourself into rivers."

She shook her head impatiently. "I wasn't trying to jump."

"Really? You were doing a pretty good imitation of a bridge jumper."

"No, I was just looking for my things." She looked away distractedly. "He…he threw them over the side of the bridge and…" Her voice trailed off and she met his gaze again, her own eyes hooded. "Never mind," she said, hunching deeper into her jacket and turning away.

He'd only heard half her muffled words but he was willing to join in. "What were you looking for? Maybe I can help you."

"No." She seemed to be trying to put distance between them. Glancing at him sideways, she began to move away. "You can't help me."

It was dark. He was large. And male. He knew he probably looked threatening to her. He didn't mean to. But what the hell? He had better things to do with his time than to follow a crazy woman around. So he shrugged.

"Fine. Have it your way."

She glanced back over her shoulder. "I will, thank you."

He slowed, then came to a stop and watched as

she hurried away. He supposed it was best to leave her alone, just as she'd demanded. Still, he hated to do it. She bothered him. There was something in the way she moved, to quote an old song.

Besides, this town was only a few months into recovering from a war and the place was crawling with unsavory characters who had nothing better to do than to make trouble for someone else. It was a problem he and his brothers were going to have to deal with very quickly. One of many. And right now it could be a problem for this troubled lady.

You can't save them all.

Those words echoed painfully in his head and he shook them away. Gordon Greiva, his best friend and comrade-in-arms, had said that often in the old days when they'd been fighting for their country's liberation. *Nico, let it go. You can't save them all.* The irony was, Gordon himself had died in that final battle.

No, he couldn't save them all. Truth to tell, he didn't have the greatest track record in saving much of any of them. And what could he do to help this one? Not much. She'd certainly made it clear she didn't want his help.

With a careless shrug, he turned away and started back toward the other side of the bridge. He needed a drink.

He heard the pub before he saw it, music and laughter an appealing invitation to step into the crowd. But he hesitated in the doorway, peering inside. He would love to go in, order Scotch, neat, and sit back and let that liquid fire burn its way into his soul, restoring him to something resembling real feeling again. It was tempting. He could see himself sitting there in the darkened room, letting the smoke and conversation wash around him while he contemplated life and all its twists and turns.

But he knew that picture was a fantasy. As soon as he sat down, the waitress would look at him sharply, then whisper to one of the other customers. The buzz would begin as people craned their necks, staring, until finally someone would get brave enough to come over and start talking. And once the ice had been broken, the flood would come, people wanting to rehash the war, people wanting to know why everything wasn't instantly wonderful now that the good guys had taken over again. And who knew if it was a bar full of patriots or a refuge for disgruntled losers. You paid your money and you took your chances. But tonight, he didn't feel up to testing those waters.

Turning away from the pub, he looked back at the river. He couldn't seem to shake the image of his distressed jumper, her wild curls floating around her face, her dark eyes filled with mystery. He wondered if she'd found what she'd been looking for, and if she was going to have any trouble making her way home. The bridge looked ominous from this angle, like a path into dangerous territory. The wet streets were empty. It was getting late and time for him to make a decision as to where he was going to spend the next few hours.

He started down the walkway that fronted the river feeling vaguely uneasy, his hands shoved deep into his pockets, his gaze running restlessly over the scene. And then it sharpened. Something was moving down by the riverbank, where various debris was piled up around a short pier. He stopped and looked harder, then swore softly and vaulted over the river wall to get to the water's edge. It was her.

A few quick strides brought him to where she was bending over a large black plastic bag.

"What the hell are you doing?" he demanded.

She looked up, startled once again. Straightening, she pushed at her damp hair, leaving wet strands plastered to her forehead. "It's none of your business."

She'd been crying. Once he saw the tears on her cheeks, he knew he was a goner. It *was* none of his business, but there was no way he could stay out of it now. She was far too vulnerable. Only a cad would leave a woman like this to fend for herself in the night.

Still, his impulse was to growl and start ordering her about. He restrained it. He knew enough about women to know that wasn't going to work out well. Taking a deep breath, he said carefully, "Why don't you tell me what you're doing. What's wrong?"

She stared at him for a moment, then shook her head. "Please, just go. I'm really busy here. I've got to find…" Her voice trailed off and she went back to trying to move the huge plastic bag.

Instead of leaving, he moved closer. "You've got to find what?"

She shook her head and threw a hand out as though covering the waterfront. "My bag. My things."

He frowned. She could hardly be talking about this big plastic bag she seemed to be so intent on moving out of the way. He reached around her and moved it for her, revealing only more, smaller plastic bags, all filled with suspicious substances. It was obviously trash someone had stacked there, along with things that had washed up on the shore.

"What sort of bag?" he asked her. "What did it look like?"

She straightened and looked around, her

bottom lip caught by her teeth, her eyes worried. "I…I'm not sure…"

He resisted the impulse to throw up his hands. "Then how are you going to find it?"

Tears welled in her dark eyes and she turned her head away, her damp curls flopping limply against her neck in a way that somehow touched him. He could see her finely cut profile against the lights from across the river. Her features were delicate, yet strong in a determined sort of way. Her body was slender despite the pregnancy. Her legs were long and exotic, like a dancer's, and her short skirt showed them off in a way that would turn any man's head. She moved like a dancer, smooth, fluid motion, like a song brought to life. But that thought made him want to laugh at himself for thinking it. He wasn't usually quite so sentimental.

Then she turned and his gaze dropped to her full breasts and the way they strained against the soft sweater she wore under her jacket, and he felt a reaction so quick and so hard, it threw him off guard for a moment.

"I don't need help," she said, but her voice quavered and the tears were still in her eyes.

Something caught in his chest and he grimaced. No, he wasn't going to let her get to him. At the same time, she obviously couldn't be abandoned here. He'd already noticed someone skulking farther down along the river. No, he was going to make sure she got to safety— wherever that might be.

But he wasn't going to care. Never again. That part of him was gone—and good riddance.

"Just go away," she said, wiping her eyes with her sleeve. "Just go."

"I'm afraid to leave you here," he shot back. "You might try another shot at river-rafting."

She glared at him. "I was *not* trying to jump into the river."

"Really? Then what were you doing? Practicing high-bar techniques for Olympic trials in gymnastics?"

She didn't answer, turning away instead.

"I'll admit it seems unlikely for someone in your condition…."

"Condition?" she asked. Then she looked down and gasped softly, her hands going protectively to her rounded belly. "Oh. I forgot."

"Forgot?"

He stared at her. Females didn't "forget" pregnancy. There was something very odd about this woman. But something distracted him from the subject. For the first time he noticed there was something dark and shiny in her hair. He touched it and drew back his fingers. Blood.

"Hey. What's this?"

She reached up but didn't quite touch it herself. "I don't know." She frowned. "Maybe I hit my head when I fell. Or...or..." She looked up at him questioningly. "Maybe it's where he hit me."

Her words sent a blinding flash of outrage slashing through him. The thought of someone deliberately hurting her made him crazy for an unguarded moment.

"Who?" he demanded. "Where? What did he do to you?"

A look of regret for having mentioned it flashed across her face and she turned away. "I don't know," she said, shaking her head. "I don't know."

"Wait." He grabbed her arm to stop her from starting off. "This is serious. I'm taking you to the police."

She jerked from his grip and began to back away, her eyes wide. "No, I can't do that. No." She glared at him, shaking her head, looking fierce. "I can't go to the police."

"Why not?"

She hesitated, looking past him.

He frowned. He could think of only two reasons why someone wouldn't want to go to the police, neither of them good.

"Look, I'll be with you. I'll handle things. There's nothing to be afraid of."

She flashed him a scathing look. "It must be nice to be so sure and cavalier about other peoples' lives," she said. "Who do you think you are, anyway? King of Carnethia?"

He looked at her sharply, but no, she really

didn't seem to know she was talking to someone pretty close to that mark.

"Just someone trying to help you," he said softly.

"Really?" She tossed her damp hair and sent him a penetrating look. "And what do you expect to get out of it?"

He gave her a half shrug and a well-practiced look of pure boredom. "I was hoping for a simple thank you, but even that seems to be out of the question."

For just a moment, her gaze faltered. "Why should I trust you?" she asked, pushing hair back out of her eyes.

"You don't seem to have a lot of choice, do you?" he grumbled, moving restlessly. "Look, if you don't want to go to the police, there must be somebody I can call to come get you or something." He pulled out his cell phone and held it poised. "Give me a number."

She shook her head and looked away.

"Come on. We've got to get you out of this drizzle, at least." He looked back at the store-fronts along the riverside. It was late and most of the shops were closed. "How about that little café there? It'll be warm and dry."

She looked up. He could see she was tempted.

"A nice hot cup of coffee? Come on. I'm buying."

She glanced at the café and a look of longing came into her face. "I'm so hungry," she admitted softly.

He snapped the cell phone shut and put it back in his pocket. "That does it. Come on. Let's go."

Turning, she looked searchingly into his face. He wondered what she saw there—a helpful new friend or the hard-bitten man he knew he'd become? It seemed she hadn't recognized who he was. That was a relief. So she wasn't particularly political. Good.

"Let's go," he said again, putting his hand lightly at her back to urge her along.

He entered the café warily, scanning the scene like a soldier on point. Simple booths lined one side of the room. Wrought-iron tables and chairs filled the center. Posters and advertisements covered the walls and pop music was playing on the speaker. The place was almost empty. A pair of young lovers had a booth at the back but they were lost in each other's eyes and paying no attention. An elderly couple was finishing up a meal toward the front. Involved in some sort of argument, neither looked up. That left the waitress and she just looked bored and very sleepy. No one reacted.

Who knew—maybe he was becoming unrecognizable. That would certainly be an improvement.

He led her to a booth in a protected corner and sat across the table from her.

"An omelet and a tall glass of milk," he ordered for her, giving the bored waitress a quick, cool smile. "And I'll take a cup of espresso."

"Eggs," the mystery woman said thoughtfully, as though she were considering whether she really liked them or not. "Okay." She sneaked a look back at the counter. "But that pie looked awfully good," she mentioned.

He stifled the grin that threatened to soften his mouth. "Okay. A large piece of the apple pie, à la mode, too. We'll share it."

As the waitress left with their order, the woman gazed at him wide-eyed with that searching look again.

"Do I know you?" she asked softly.

He looked at her sharply, afraid she'd realized who he was, but all he saw was bewilderment in her beautiful eyes, and he relaxed. If she felt he looked familiar, but couldn't quite place who he was, that might at least make her trust him a bit more.

"Not that I know of," he replied lightly. "We met on the bridge just tonight."

"Ah. Of course."

"And I don't know your name," he noted.

She nodded as though she thoroughly agreed, and he prodded further.

"My name's Nick," he said, fudging a bit. "What's yours?"

"Uh…" She looked trapped for a moment and avoided his gaze, looking about the café as though she was going to find the answer to his question in the atmosphere. "Marisa," she said quickly as her eyes focused behind his head. "It's Marisa. Marisa Fleur."

"Marisa," he repeated. "Pretty name." He stuck out his hand. "Nice to meet you, Marisa."

She put her small, fine-boned hand in his and for the first time, she actually smiled. "Nice to meet you, too, Nick."

The beat of his heart stuttered. There was no way to deny it. For just a second, he was afraid his heart had stopped. The feel of her small, smooth hand in his, the beauty of her sweet smile, the warmth that came momentarily from her dark gaze, all combined to shock him as though someone had hit him with a stun dart. He blinked, drew in a sharp breath, and quickly pulled his hand away from hers. *What the hell...?*

"And thank you," she was saying. "It might not seem like it but I really appreciate you taking the time to...well, to help me."

He nodded, avoiding her gaze, still shaken by the involuntary reaction he'd had to her smile and touch. "No problem," he said gruffly.

He risked looking at her and it was okay. Whatever spell had swept over him seemed to be gone for now. Still, forewarned was forearmed. He was going to be on his guard from now on.

He waited for her to take a few bites of her omelet before trying to question her. Her color was better by then, and she'd lost most of that trapped look.

"So," he said, nursing his espresso in both hands. "Are you ready to tell me what happened?"

She looked up at him, eyes wide. "You mean on the bridge?" she asked.

He nodded.

She looked down. "I…well, I think a man came up from behind and knocked me down."

His hand tightened on the slender cup. "Did you know him?"

"I don't think so. No," she amended quickly. "No, I'm sure he was just a mugger or something. He grabbed my purse and then he threw my bag over the side of the bridge." She gazed at him earnestly. "That's why I was climbing up on the railing. I was trying to see where my bag had gone."

"And that was what you were looking for along the side of the river?"

She nodded. "I know there's not much hope in finding my purse, but if I could find my bag…"

"It's a suitcase?"

She hesitated, looking uncertain. Then she nodded again.

He frowned. There was something odd and off-kilter about all this. "When did it happen?"

She hesitated, shrugged, then her eyes lit up as she remembered. "Just before I saw you the first time. I think maybe you scared him away."

The waitress brought them a huge slice of pie on a ceramic plate. A rounded mound of vanilla ice cream was melting on top. Marisa smiled again and he frowned to keep from letting it get to him.

"So you're here from out of town?" he noted as he handed her a fork. "Where are you from?"

She looked down again. "I really can't talk about that," she said evasively.

He shrugged. "Do you know anyone in town?" he asked.

She didn't answer but the look on her face said it all. What was he going to do with her? The realization came to him with a sick feeling in the pit of his stomach. He was going to take her home. At this time of night, what else could he do?

They rose to leave and he turned to let her go first, and as he did so, his gaze fell on an advertising poster on the wall behind where he'd been sitting. Marisa's Flowers it said, along with an address and telephone number.

Marisa's Flowers. He turned slowly and watched as she walked ahead of him out of the café, and that feeling in the pit of his stomach got sicker.

CHAPTER TWO

MARISA.

It wasn't her name but it felt like a near fit. Close enough—for now. Her real name was there, right on the tip of her tongue, but every time she thought she had it, it slipped away again. But it would come. She had no doubt about that. She'd hit her head pretty hard and it had knocked her silly for a moment. Give her a little time and a bit of rest and it would all come back. If only she could find her suitcase....

She glanced at the man walking beside her. He was near thirty, large and hard and there was something just a little bit dangerous about him. There was something appealing, too, despite his icy demeanor. But she needed to be careful. She'd been wrong about men before. Hadn't she? She couldn't think exactly how, but she knew it was true. She wasn't thinking too clearly right now but she did know one thing: men were nothing but trouble. She'd best get away from this one as soon as possible.

"Thanks for the late-night snack," she said, keeping her tone light. "I'm sure you've got places to go and people to meet, so I'll just say goodbye here."

She stuck out her hand. He took it but not for the handshake she'd expected.

"Where are you going?" he said, looking down at her, his hand warm on hers.

She tugged, but he wasn't letting go. Looking up, she winced—partly at how tall he was, but mostly for the look of resolve in his silver-blue eyes. The man wasn't going to go gently into the dark and foggy night, was he?

She hesitated. What she really wanted to do was get back to looking for her suitcase. She needed that bag with an urgency she wasn't really clear on—but she needed it badly. She wanted to comb both sides of the river until it turned up. But something told her he wasn't going to go for that.

"I know where I'm going," she said quickly. "You don't have to worry about me. I've got… uh…someplace to stay."

He cocked one dark eyebrow, and it was the sexiest thing she'd ever seen a man do. She gaped at him, astonished at her own reaction. He was masculine magic—a gangster right out of a thirties film, a movie star dining at the Copa in the forties, a military commander from the fifties, a rock star from the sixties, Italian royalty from any decade at all. He had the presence common to all those icons, a sort of magnificent sense of command that took her breath away.

And he didn't believe a word she'd said, making her shiver with the sort of expectant chill she only got from a really good thriller.

"Fine," he was saying as she was pulling herself back down to earth. "I'll go with you to make sure you get to your destination without any more bridge diversions."

She felt that under ordinary circumstances, she

would have talked back and insisted on going her own way, but she was still getting over the shock his insolent eyebrow had given her, so she nodded and began to make her way along the riverfront sidewalk, her companion beside her, and not an idea in her head as to where she would go.

She had to make up her mind soon. They couldn't just wander around the city. She bit her lip and tried to think of some way to get into a doorway that would pass muster as her final objective.

Meanwhile, they walked.

It was late and the streets were deserted, but there was a man in the block ahead, leaning against the wall of a building, playing his guitar. As they got closer, she could see that he was standing near the entrance to a sort of nightclub. Music and laughter floated out, but the man was playing to his own muse, standing under a light. He wore dark glasses and there was a cup on the ground near his feet. Maybe he was blind.

Maybe. But she shivered. Something about him…

Maybe it was just the night. As her mother used to say, *nothing good happens out there after midnight.*

Her mother? She tried to grab hold of that concept, tried to see a face, but it slipped away before she could focus. A feeling of loss filled her, but she tamped it down. Never mind, she would think of it soon enough.

Turning to her companion as they reached the crosswalk, she put her hand on his arm. "Let's go this way," she said, nodding down a direction that would avoid the guitar player. "I think this is quicker."

He came along without comment and in a moment or two, she was breathing evenly again. Funny. She didn't know why, but the man playing his guitar on the previous block had reminded her of something…something she didn't want to remember.

Which shouldn't be a surprise, she supposed wryly. After all, she wasn't remembering much. Was this going to be a long-term problem? Possibly. But right now it was mostly annoying.

And her mind was full of so many things, she didn't have time to worry about it.

The first order of business was to get rid of this man so she could go back and find her suitcase. Something told her that was the key to getting herself back to normal. As they came to another corner, she stopped and smiled at him quickly.

"There it is," she said, gesturing down the block. "I can handle the rest of this on my own," she added breezily. "Thanks again."

She turned to hurry off, but his hand stopped that, his long fingers curling around her upper arm.

"Marisa," he said, a smile teasing the corners of his wide mouth as he looked down into her wide eyes, "this is Embassy Row."

She turned and looked. Sure enough, the street was lined with stately mansions, and even in the dark, she could see the placards identifying the countries.

"So?" she said, trying to remain nonchalant. "I...I'm staying with the Hungarians for now." She looked up to see if he was buying it.

He laughed shortly. "Liar," he said calmly.

"The Hungarian embassy has been closed down for years and they haven't sent a new delegation yet." He shrugged. "Want to try again?"

She glared at him. He was becoming insufferable.

"Look, I don't want to argue about this. I appreciate your concern, but you have no hold over me." Very deliberately, she peeled away his fingers, making a graphic statement to back up her words. "And I'd like to be on my own."

"You can't be."

She wrinkled her nose, frowning up at him. "What are you talking about?"

That wonderful eyebrow rose again. "You're carrying a baby with you, no matter what you do," he said flatly. "And that means you need to take a little extra care, don't you think?"

Looking down, she bit her lip. He was right. She could see the slight bulge of her tummy. She was pregnant! It startled her every time she remembered. How had this happened?

Well, she supposed it was in the usual way. Still, you'd think she would remember something like that. At least, she should remember the man involved.

She wished her mind would clear. She was so confused. She knew it would be crazy to go with this man she didn't even know. Of course, in some ways it was even crazier to go roaming the streets when she didn't know where to go or what to ask for. What was she going to do, sleep under a bridge or in a doorway like a homeless person?

But that seemed to be what she was right now. Until she figured out who she was and where she was going, she was homeless.

"I'll be honest with you, Marisa," he went on. "You're a grown woman. If you want to wander the streets of this city at all hours, ordinarily you could be my guest. But right now, things are different. You've got to think about that baby you're carrying."

She blinked at him, not sure where he was going with this.

He considered her levelly. "I think you'd better come home with me."

That shocked her. She gasped softly, wondering if he really meant it—and how he meant it. What kind of a home was he talking about? What sort of situation?

She looked up with a wry smile. "What will your wife think?" she tried, fishing for information.

A cold shadow passed through his gaze. "I'm not married."

She shivered, then tried to make light of the circumstances with a quip. "That's what they all say. Right after they claim to read *Playboy* for the articles."

His mouth twisted. Despite himself, he almost grinned. "Okay," he admitted, "I'll plead guilty to being male."

She wondered if that meant he was acknowledging a certain attraction. She thought maybe it did, and that made her want to smile, too. Better to make a smart-aleck crack instead, she decided hurriedly.

"Wise move," she retorted with a nod. "Next you might as well throw yourself on the mercy of the court. That'll get you a lighter sentence."

"If you're the court, I'd think twice," he shot back. "But either way, here's the truth. I'm not married."

He wasn't married. Was she? No, she didn't think so. Despite the fact that she was pregnant, she couldn't picture herself married. It just didn't feel like it.

She studied him with her head to the side, considering. "Do you have any children?" She only asked because he seemed so concerned about the baby she was carrying.

"No. But I care a lot about children. And I think it's only fair to give a baby the best first nine months you possibly can."

She nodded. Of course she agreed. Who wouldn't? But what did that mean, exactly? If she couldn't even remember why she was pregnant….

"Come on," he said, starting off across the street. "You're dead on your feet. We've got to have a doctor look at you before you pass out."

"Doctor?" She found herself going along with him again. What had happened to her determined effort to peel off? It seemed to have melted into the mist. "Where are you going to find a doctor at this time of night?"

"I've got one where I live."

That made her do a double take. "Really?"

"Yes." He glanced at her sideways, a half grin just for her. "I've also got a sister who will take care of you. So you don't have to worry about my intentions."

She wanted to protest, to say she hadn't been a bit worried, but the words stuck in her throat.

"Once we get there, I probably won't even see you again. Carla will handle everything."

"Will she?" He was walking quickly now and she was hurrying just to keep up.

"Yes. She's capable of handling just about anything. The entire country, even."

"Well, if she can handle you, I'm sold."

They stopped at the crosswalk on a major road. Two cars sped past. Looking back, she thought she saw someone duck between two buildings. That gave her a start, then she relaxed. She was imagining things. This night was taking a toll on her sanity, wasn't it? She felt an overwhelming need to bring things to rights as much as she could.

Nico took her arm. "We're almost there," he told her.

Instead of starting off across the street, she hung back, putting her own hand on his.

"Okay, listen," she said seriously. "Before we get there, I've got a confession to make."

His eyes darkened as he looked down into hers. "Really."

"Yes." Taking a deep breath, she closed her own eyes for a moment, then opened them and blurted out, "I don't know where I'm going or what I'm doing."

He almost smiled. "That's been obvious from the first moment I saw you."

She pressed her hand on his and gazed earnestly up into his eyes. "No, I'm serious. I really don't know who I am."

He blinked and the smile faded. "That's why you made up that name, Marisa Fleur?"

She gasped. "How did you know?"

He shrugged. "I saw the sign in the café and figured it out pretty quickly."

She sighed, shoulders slumping. "I wish I was a better liar," she muttered.

"What was the point of lying?" he said sensibly. "You got hit on the head and you're a little confused. That's why you need to see a doctor."

She looked at him in surprise, then realized what he saw when he looked at her. He saw a woman under suspicion of wanting to commit suicide. Maybe he thought she'd wanted to jump because she was pregnant and had no husband. And why wouldn't he think that? She had no wedding ring on her finger. That made her bite her lip. She probably wasn't married, but she really didn't know. And why was her impulse to lie about it all? Was she trying to hide something?

But all that was crazy. She wasn't suicidal. She was confused, but not ready to end it all. Was she?

No, of course not. Why couldn't she keep things straight? She'd climbed up on the bridge to try to see where the man had tossed her suitcase. She had hoped to see where it had landed, or where the river might have taken it, so that she could get it back and find her things and clear everything up. That was all. Nothing earth-shaking. She hoped.

"Come on," he said. "I live right across the street."

She looked at where he was pointing and gasped. "Wait a minute. Isn't this Altamere? The royal palace?"

"Yes. Come along." He started across the street and she came along willingly, gaping at the huge Gothic building they were headed for.

"Oh my," she said softly.

He glanced down at her. "Have you been here before?"

"What? No. I don't think so. But…" She looked at him questioningly as he used a remote to open the huge iron gates. "Do you work here or something?"

"No, Marisa," he said, closing the gates behind them and nodding to a security guard. "I live here."

"Wait." Grabbing his arm, she stopped and stared up at him, her eyes huge with wonder. "Ohmigod. You're one of the princes, aren't you?"

He smiled, his blue eyes shining with amusement. "Guilty as charged."

That did it. The world started to swirl and if Nico hadn't caught her, she would have hit the ground for the second time that night.

CHAPTER THREE

"ALL I can say is, it's about time you brought a woman home."

Nico turned to throw a stern glance at his lively, dark-haired sister as she entered the parlor where he'd taken Marisa just after she'd fainted in his arms. But his next words were directed at the silent-as-a-ghost butler standing near the door.

"Chauncy, has Dr. Zavier been contacted?"

"Yes, Your Highness," the man responded with a slight bow. "He is on his way here now."

"Good."

He turned back to Marisa, looking down at her, where she lay on the velveteen couch, with a frown of concern. She hadn't stirred since he'd carried her in. Did that have any connection to the bump on the head she'd taken earlier on the bridge? He took her hand in his again and felt her pulse. She was lying very still with her eyes closed, but he couldn't see any other evidence of injury. Her breathing was normal.

What the hell—maybe she was asleep.

"She's very pretty," Carla noted, leaning on his shoulder to look at the exceptionally pretty blond woman. "Though I thought brunettes were more your type."

He had to bite back the sharp retort that rose in his throat. Maybe Carla had forgotten about Andrea.

Andrea. Just thinking her name slashed another jagged tear into his heart. A vision of wild, lustrous auburn curls filled his mind's eye. Memories of her dancing green eyes, her soft skin, her rolling laughter swept over him in a wave that threatened to choke him. He pulled away from his sister and began to pace the Persian carpet, fighting back the crippling anger that always came when he thought of his loss.

Marisa was a very different type. Slender and

light, her blond hair curling into an impenetrable mass that didn't quite reach her shoulders, she was nothing like the woman he had loved. But just seeing Marisa lying there on the couch brought back his most painful memories.

Andrea had been on the cold, hard ground that awful night, over a year ago now. They'd been pinned down by a sniper and his rounds were still biting in around them as he'd worked frantically on her wounds. Ripping apart his shirt to use to bind her torn flesh, he tried desperately to stop the bleeding. He cried out encouragement, prayed aloud, promised things and begged. But the blood kept coming, slowly draining her life away. And finally, there was nothing to do but to cradle her lifeless body in his arms and curse and sob out his anguish and promise revenge.

But that was then. This was now. And the woman on the couch wasn't in danger of dying. Still, she was alone and vulnerable and she carried a child, just like Andrea. He couldn't ignore the parallels.

"This is hardly a date, Carla," he rebuked her

curtly, just because he had to funnel his anguish into anger in order to keep it under control.

"Well, brother dear, it's as close as you've come lately," she said cheerfully, pushing back her thick black hair and bending over Marisa.

He glanced over, regretting that he'd snapped at her, though not quite enough actually to apologize. He knew it hadn't been easy for Carla, growing up during a war with three older brothers always taking precedence. He should cut her some slack.

Carla had lived a strange, schizoid existence, sometimes thrust into the midst of bloody battles as the family fled attack, at other times treated as though she were the proverbial pampered princess to be kept away from ordinary life as long as possible. Their mother had died two years ago and their father, the king, very recently. When she'd been alive their mother had always acted as though Carla's primary role in life was to wait for the right eligible swain to present his credentials and get permission to sweep her off her feet. So Carla had waited. But the war and other things had cluttered the time up and now, in her early twenties, he knew she was beginning to fear she had waited too long.

Seeing the look in his eyes, Carla knew he was thinking about her situation. She appreciated his compassion, but a little action on her behalf would be more useful. Princesses were usually betrothed by now. And no one seemed to be doing anything about it.

When she'd taken her fears to their aunt Kitty, the older woman had reassured her.

"Don't worry, dear," she'd said, patting her hand lovingly. "I'm sure your brothers will always need looking after. If you don't get married, there will always be a place for you at the palace."

It had been a shock to realize her aunt didn't think much of her chances either. If only she'd been born beautiful, the way her brothers were handsome, things would have been so much easier. She wasn't bitter, but it did seem unfair.

"You seem beautiful to me," her father had always said, but that, obviously, didn't help at all.

She'd decided, if it came down to it, she would

run away to another country, change her identity and join a dressage team training for the Olympics. Why not? She was good at working with horses. Better that than feeling like a piece of furniture half of the time.

The woman Nico had settled onto the couch was beautiful. Carla smiled as she looked her over. She was as happy to admire beauty as the next person. But as she looked, she noticed the woman's rounded stomach.

"Uh-oh. It looks like she's got a little traveler along for the ride." She shook her head, frowning. "Darn. Does that mean she's already married?"

The prince moved away restlessly. "I'm not really sure about that."

"Oh?" She straightened and gazed at him questioningly.

He shoved his hands down into the pockets of his slacks. "She's…well, it's a bit complicated, but she got mugged tonight and now it seems she's not sure who she is."

"Amnesia?" Carla's silver-blue eyes, so like Nico's, glittered with interest.

"Maybe."

Carla turned back to look at her. "No traditional rings." She tilted her head, considering
the silent woman. "I'd say she's unattached."

"Carla…" he said warningly.

"But then, I'm an optimist." She allowed
herself a quick look of concern before she went
back to needling her brother. "Of course, you've
as good a chance as anyone at turning her head."

He groaned.

"But that doesn't explain why she fainted."
Turning, she gave him an arch look. "You've obviously terrified the poor dear. What on earth did
you do to her?"

"Nothing at all," he said defensively. "She
just…well, when she realized who I was…"

Carla laughed and threw up her hands. "Of
course. That would be enough to scare any girl
into a stupor."

He turned away with a snort. "Where's that
damn doctor?"

"He was probably sound asleep when Chauncy
called him," Carla said, getting a confirming nod

from the butler. The doctor's house, where he lived with his wife and the two nieces they'd taken in when they had been orphaned, was at the far edge of the compound. "It is after midnight. Don't worry, he'll get here." She smiled as she watched her brother go back to pacing the floor.

Marisa was lying very still, her eyes closed, her mind drifting. If she stayed very quiet, maybe she could pretend she was asleep and dreaming and she could put off the reality of her situation. The murmured voices of the others in the room were muted, washing around her. Still, try as she might, she couldn't help but hear what they were saying.

It was all a little too much right now. Somehow she had walked out of her own everyday reality and stepped into a fantasy—she'd just been carried into a palace in the arms of a prince, for heaven's sake! And she couldn't even remember how or why she got here.

Carefully, she tried to reconstruct her day, but she couldn't remember anything that had happened before she found herself on the cold bridge walkway with a lump on her head. She'd tried to shake off the dizziness and she was aware of a man throwing her suitcase and purse over the side of the bridge. What had happened to him? By the time she'd regained her feet, she'd noticed Nico coming toward her and the man who'd attacked her was nowhere to be seen.

The rest was a muddle of clearing her head and walking along with the man she now knew was Prince Nico. There was a stop for something to eat in a café, but what had happened there was blurry. And then the prince had brought her here.

He and his sister were talking as though they didn't think she could hear a thing they were saying. She knew she ought to open her eyes and sit up and join in, but she still needed a moment or two to regroup. Just a moment or two.

"Be serious for a minute," the prince was saying, reacting in exasperation to something his sister had said. "And tell me what we're going to do with her."

"Don't think twice, Nico. I've already got the second-floor maids up, running a bath, preparing the peach room, laying out nightclothes."

His tone turned reluctantly admiring. "I have to admit, you're nothing if not efficient."

"I do my best. Just trying to make sure that your little treasure has a place to lay her head."

"Excuse me, Your Highness."

Marisa frowned slightly at the new voice that was practically a whisper, then realized it was the butler.

"Yes, Chauncy?"

"I hesitate to intrude, but I thought it might be wise to point out another factor that might have upset the young lady."

"And what is that?" Nico sounded just a bit impatient and she could see why. The man sounded conniving to her, too.

"We live in perilous times, Your Highness. I don't think you can afford to rule out the possibility that she might be…affiliated with the opposition in some way and was shocked to find herself ensconced with the enemy, so to speak."

"Nonsense. Chauncy, you see enemies behind every bush."

"Of course, Your Highness. I beg your pardon for speaking so candidly."

Marisa lay very still and wondered if she was part of the opposition. She didn't know the answer to that question, but she did know she had to get out of here. Carla had called her a treasure. What on earth had she meant by that? Unbidden, an old Carnethian folk song trailed its way into her mind. The refrain repeated, "Oh what a lucky girl, to be the prince's plaything." The phrase was said with bitter irony and added a bad feeling to this crazy mix. Royalty played exotic games in a rarified atmosphere she wasn't used to. She didn't belong here.

And something was tugging at her—some responsibility she hadn't met, or some errand she hadn't completed. She had to go, even if she didn't know where.

Reluctantly, she opened her eyes, just as the doctor arrived, but it was the prince's gaze she met first. The connection that sparked between them made her gasp softly. She hadn't realized before just how blue those eyes were, or how provocative. She saw something there that set off alarms inside her and sent her heart into a thumping frenzy. But maybe she was imagining things, because a moment later his look was cool and impassive and he was speaking to the doctor as though she were a homeless person he'd found in the street. Which she was, wasn't she?

The only time he revealed a flash of emotion was when the doctor turned to him almost accusingly.

"This woman is pregnant," he said, looking sternly at the prince.

Nico's face hardened and he stared at the man. "I just met her tonight," he said icily.

It was obvious the two men didn't care much for each other, but Marisa didn't have time to dwell on that fact. Dr. Zavier examined her quickly and dispassionately, then declared her well enough for now. He found nothing physically wrong, other than a bump on the head, and prescribed lots of rest and plenty of fluids and promised to look in on her in the morning.

Marisa agreed with that diagnosis. She was fine, really. Just tired and a bit confused. She sat up as the doctor left, then looked hesitantly into the prince's eyes, wary of seeing whatever that was she'd seen a few moments before, but his gaze was bland, revealing nothing more than vaguely impatient interest, and she relaxed. She was probably being a ninny and she hated that. Squaring her shoulders, she resolved to be stronger from now on. Just as soon as that was possible.

Nico introduced her to Carla, his sister, who immediately took over and ushered her down the hall and up the stairs and into a warm bath, chattering in a friendly manner all the while. Two chambermaids helped and Marisa didn't have to do a thing. Before she knew it, she was clean and smelling delicious with her dirt-stained clothes exchanged for a silky nightdress that felt like heaven. And finally, Carla led her to a luxuriously plush canopied bed in a beautiful room decorated in peach and gold. By the time Marisa had caught her breath, she knew it was all too much.

"I should go," she protested weakly, knowing she was in danger of letting herself be seduced by all this cosseting.

"Nonsense," Carla told her cheerfully, turning back the bed and providing a stepstool. "It's late. You need to sleep. You can go in the morning."

"But, my clothes…"

"They're being cleaned for you. In the meantime, look here." Carla threw open a tall wardrobe set against the inner wall. "You see all these?" she said, sweeping her hand along the length of the display inside. Bright cloth hung from every hanger. "They belong to my cousin Nadia. She's just about your age and size. Minus the pregnancy, of course, but you're barely showing. Feel free to use anything here that you like."

Marisa shivered. This was beginning to remind her of a fairy tale. Fairy tales didn't always have happy endings. She could think of a few where the young innocent visitor was lulled into a false sense of security by all the riches laid before her, only to come to a bad end when she finally realized what the evil captors actually wanted from her.

"Uh, where *is* Nadia?" she asked.

Carla shrugged and pretty much evaded a straight answer. "Good question. That's something we'd all like to know."

She drew the heavy drapes closed over the lacy liners at the window and Marisa turned slowly, following her movements. She was hesitant to seem to be looking a gift horse in the mouth, but still….

"I… I don't really know why you're being so nice to me," she said carefully. "I mean, you don't know anything about me or where I came from or…"

Carla's good-natured laugh rang out. "Well, neither do you, from what I hear. We're all playing this by ear, aren't we?"

Marisa couldn't help but return her smile. "I guess you're right," she said reluctantly.

"You get into that bed and get some sleep," Carla said, turning to go. "There's a bell rope if you need anything."

"Carla," Marisa said quickly, "thank you."

Carla stopped at the doorway and looked back. She hesitated, then sighed. "I'll be honest, Marisa. It's lovely having you here, but the bottom line is that Nico is in charge when our oldest brother, Crown Prince Dane, is out of town. I'm sure you know—but then, maybe you've forgotten—that our father, King Nevander, died last month after a long illness. So now we're preparing for a coronation. The Crown Prince is in Paris making international alliances. Nico is the de facto ruler here at home for the time being. And Nico gets what he wants. If he thinks you're welcome here, you're welcome here. So relax and enjoy it."

With a wave she was gone. Marisa stared after her. Somehow her last words had not been comforting. The more she heard the prince wanted her here, the more she began to think she didn't want to be here. Instead of heading for the bed, she turned and hurried toward the wardrobe, reaching in to grab something to wear for a quick escape. She'd barely taken down a beautiful pink sweater when a soft rapping on her door told her this wasn't going to be quite so easy.

"Come in," she said, tensed in uneasy anticipation.

Prince Nico entered the room, just as she'd been afraid he would. Funny, but he looked more handsome, taller, harder and just a bit scarier than he had when she hadn't known he was royal. Biting her lip hard, she tried to hold back any evidence of being swept away. She absolutely refused to seem awestruck. She'd been impressed with him before, but once she realized he was royalty—like it or not, that had its effect. The royals were stars. How could it be any other way?

"How are you feeling?" he asked, gazing curiously at the pink sweater.

"I'm fine. Absolutely fine." She pressed the sweater to her chest. "I…listen, I'm sorry to be such a bother to everyone." She gazed up at him earnestly. "Really. I think I should go. You know…"

His handsome face was impassive but his

blue eyes shimmered silver in the lamplight. "You can't go."

"Oh." That startled her for a moment. Why couldn't she go? It didn't make any sense. Was he just throwing his royal weight around? Or did he have some ulterior motive? She wasn't sure why she was so suspicious of everyone. But then again, maybe she did have a hint or two as to why that might be. After all, she'd been assaulted tonight. Time to guard herself a bit more carefully, perhaps.

"Well, I'm sure you have better things to do than to look after me. I mean…here you are, a prince and all." She shook her head and tried to convince him. "If I'd realized that from the beginning, I would never have gotten…" The word *involved* was the one she was going for, but the connotations scared her off. "…tangled up with you," she said instead, then frowned, wondering if maybe that was worse.

The faintest of smiles quirked the corners of his mouth. "Too late. I'm entangled." Reaching out, he took the hanger with the pink sweater from her hands and walked it back to the wardrobe.

She gazed at him, nonplussed. "But why?"

He hung up the sweater, then closed the door and turned back. "That doesn't matter."

Her warning system was setting off tiny alarms again. "Sure it does. I don't understand why you think you have any responsibility for me and my child."

He gazed at her for a long moment before answering that one—long enough that she began to feel self-conscious. She *was* standing there in a filmy nightdress, after all. Hardly the way one would want to appear in an audience with a prince. Unless, of course, one had seduction in mind. That sent blood rushing to her cheeks and she crossed her arms over her chest, wishing she had the sweater back to hide behind.

"We care about all our subjects, Marisa," he said at last.

Right. She almost laughed aloud at that one. Especially when she considered the hint of mockery she heard in his tone.

"Maybe so, but you don't invite them all to come and stay in the palace, do you?"

His blue eyes seemed to smile. "No. You've got me there. I'll have to admit it. You're special."

That gave her the shivers. "Why?" she demanded, though she wasn't sure she really wanted to hear the answer.

He glanced down. She knew her pregnancy was pretty well hidden by the folds of the gown, but it almost felt as though he had X-ray eyes. He was very obviously referring to her child as the reason he was taking extra care to protect her. Her hands went involuntarily to her belly once again and she bit her lip, wondering if she could trust him—or if this was just a way to lower her defenses.

"Are you married?" he asked bluntly.

"What?"

"You're pregnant. The usual order of things would require a husband somewhere in the mix."

She looked down. Funny, she couldn't remember who the father was right now—but despite the fact that there had been a moment there, when she'd still been groggy from the mugging and this amnesia or whatever it might be was still new to her, that she'd been startled to find she was with child, she was now well aware that she was carrying a baby close to her heart. She would never lose sight of that for a moment.

"I'm not married," she said firmly.

He cocked his head to the side. "Can you remember…?"

"No." She lifted her gaze to meet his. She knew instinctively that she had never voluntarily submitted to the authority of a husband. And she was beginning to feel very similarly about the authority of a prince. "But I know I'm not married. I can feel it."

He frowned. "Perhaps your husband was killed in the war."

She shook her head, chin high. "No."

His eyes darkened. "You seem very sure."

"I am. Look." She held up both hands. The simple rings she wore left no room for the traditional Carnethian doubles all married women wore in this country. "I would remember. I just can't believe I would forget a thing like that. Or if there were anyone in my life that I was in love with."

He nodded slowly. "Maybe the answer will be in your luggage. I'll send out men to search for your suitcase first thing in the morning."

Her suitcase! That sense of urgency came over her again. She looked toward the door. "I really should go," she began.

"You're not going anywhere," he cut in, sounding like a man whose patience was still holding, but not for much longer. "The doctor said you needed rest."

"Yes. But that doesn't mean I have to get it here. Look, I can take care of myself."

"I have no doubt of that. But what about your baby?"

"What about my baby?" she said defensively. "It really has nothing to do with you."

For just a moment, she thought she saw him wince, as though her feisty words had hurt him somehow. Despite everything, she regretted it. And that was a real problem. Her impulse was to do anything she could to make him happy. And that made her want to scream.

"Your Highness," she said, purposefully using his rank as a way to distance herself from him. "I may not remember my name at the moment. And I may not be too clear on where I came from."

She paused for a moment as a picture swam into her mind, a hazy, misty picture that wouldn't quite come into focus. She blinked, thinking the clouds would clear in a second or two and she would see it perfectly.

"Are you remembering something?" he asked, stepping closer.

She drew in a quick breath as the picture evaporated before her eyes. Looking at him, she twisted her mouth slightly. "Not anymore," she said coolly.

He nodded. "Let me know if you do," he said, searching her face as though he thought the answers might appear there.

She sighed. Here was the problem. He saw her as a victim, someone who needed to be taken care of. She'd been through a lot today and taken some hard knocks, but she knew one thing for sure—she was no victim. She could take care of herself. She was going to have to pull herself together enough to show him that inner toughness before it was too late.

"Get some sleep," he told her, starting to turn away. "We'll discuss your situation tomorrow. I'll see you in the morning."

"Not if I see you first," she muttered to herself as she listened to the sharp sound of his boots on the tiled floor of the hallway.

CHAPTER FOUR

MARISA stared at what she could see of the flowered canopy above her. Not much moonlight slipped in around the heavy drapes. She'd slept for an hour or so, but something was gnawing at her and she was completely awake now. If she was going to try to find a way out of this place, now was the time. She had to go. She didn't feel right being here in the first place. This memory thing was driving her crazy. She was so sure she would remember everything if only she could find her missing bag. There was a compulsion driving her. She had to hurry back to the river and find her bag before anyone else did. And the most chilling thought of all. If she never found it, would she ever remember who she was?

Sitting up, she leaned against the headboard and tried to make a plan. She was in the palace. There were guards. There were probably alarms on the windows and doors. So how was she going to get out of here?

Well…how about a bold walk right out the front door? Why would a guard even want to stop her? She was a guest in this house and she wanted to leave. What could be simpler?

Slipping out of bed, she went to the wardrobe, bypassing the pink sweater for a light training suit in more earthy tones. The pants were stretchy and fitted just fine around her belly. The top was a little snug around her bust. She was ready to go.

In moments she was making her way carefully down the wide staircase and into the dimly lit marble foyer. Catching sight of the front-door guards through the glass, she stopped and chewed on her lip. Now that she was down here, coming face to face with a couple of men likely to have overly aggressive authoritarian complexes didn't seem like such a good idea. Maybe she ought to try a side door or window first, something in one of the rooms that opened off the foyer. Turning she dismissed first one doorway, then another. A semi-dark room appeared to her left. It seemed to be a library of some sort, with floor-to-ceiling windows. Light from the moon cast a silver aspect across the floor that was almost inviting. She slipped inside, heading for the windows. Surely she would be able to open at least one of them, and if she could get through into the garden without triggering the alarm…

Prince Nico sat in semi-darkness, sunk in the depths of a huge leather chair in the palace library, a glass of amber liquid in his hand. The night was stretching out long and lonely ahead of him. He wished there was a switch that could turn his mind off. It was running like a rat in a wheel. At this rate, he was never going to be able to sleep.

The cause was plain enough. Marisa. Marisa with her amnesia and her adorable bewilderment and her strangely vulnerable eyes and her determined bravery. And most of all, with the mystery child she carried. For some reason she had appeared out of the mist and walked into his life, conjuring up all his old ghosts and setting them free to torture him once again. He had a feeling he wasn't going to be able to sleep for a long time.

And why was that? What had she done to him? There was no real reason for it. Marisa looked nothing like Andrea. Her personality was very different as well. So why had she captured his imagination like no other woman had done for a long, long time?

Throwing back his head, he groaned softly. He knew exactly what it was—he just had to face it.

First, she was pregnant and at just about the same stage Andrea had been when she'd been killed. That just naturally reached out and twisted his heart in ways not much else could. He wanted to protect her, to keep the world and all its ugliness away from her, to make sure nothing happened before she delivered her baby. His own baby had died with Andrea. A double tragedy. A double outrage. The pain had been unbearable. If he had the power, he would make sure that never happened to anyone again.

Okay, was that enough? Did that answer the questions roiling inside him? He lifted his glass and looked at the way a shaft of moonlight turned the drink inside to liquid gold and knew he hadn't begun to give a full answer.

Ah hell. He took another long sip and put the glass down on the table at his elbow. Maybe he'd had enough to drink now to be honest with himself.

"She turns me on."

There. He'd said it. And now he hated himself.

It was true. She'd stirred something in him he hadn't felt since he'd lost Andrea. Despite everything, she'd resurrected a sensual response he'd thought had been destroyed that horrible day on the mountain. He hadn't felt the slightest interest in another woman for over a year. He'd wondered, fleetingly, if maybe that part of his life had died with the woman he loved.

No more worries along that score. Every time he saw Marisa he couldn't stop looking at her mouth and wanting to taste her, wanting to cup those full, rounded breasts that strained at the material of her skimpy top in the palms of his hands. Even her rounded belly appealed to him. When he'd seen her in that filmy nightdress, her dark nipples just barely showing through the lace, he'd thought his arousal was going to be so obvious, she wouldn't be able to miss it. He wanted her in a deep, primal way that almost shocked him—the dominant male urge to stake his claim.

What the hell was wrong with him?

Closing his eyes, he let himself think about Andrea. He very rarely did that. It hurt too much. But right now he felt he needed to remind himself of what really mattered in his life. For just a moment, he saw her again, felt her again. He remembered the day she'd told him she was pregnant. He'd covered her face with kisses and they'd clung together, laughing their joy into the air, planning how it was going to be to bring a new baby into the world at the same time they were helping to usher in a new life for their country. He felt the joy again, just for a few seconds, and then her image began to slip away, like a wisp of mist, into the night. A lump rose in his throat and his eyes stung.

"Don't go," he whispered softly to himself.

He heard something. Opening his eyes, his heart lurched. There she was right in front of him! The light from the hallway made a halo effect around her body, while the moonlight lit her hair with silver.

"Andrea?" he whispered in wonder, rising from the chair.

But in that same instant, he realized who it really was. Marisa. Disappointment and then anger flashed through him, as though she'd been deliberately impersonating his lost love. He stood, barring her way, glaring at her and all she represented to him in his useless agony.

"Oh!" Marisa gasped, jumping back. He'd startled her. If she'd seen him there, she never would have come this way.

He stood in her path, immovable, looking dark and dangerous "Where exactly do you think you're going?" he demanded.

She took in a deep breath and stiffened her spine. A part of her had known he would probably find a way to try to stop her. Now that she'd spotted him, she could see a glass of liquor on the small table beside where he'd been sitting. He'd been drinking. Would that mellow him or make him more menacing?

"I want to go home," she said quickly. "I didn't want to bother you again, so…"

The words died in her throat as her eyes grew accustomed to the gloom and began to see him more clearly. He was barefoot and his shirt was unbuttoned, hanging open as though he'd begun getting ready for bed and then decided to come down here for a drink. His eyes were darkly haunted, his mouth a hard, relentless line that told her he could be cruel. But what really took her breath away was the gorgeous landscape of his hard, muscular chest. She hadn't seen muscles like that since…well, she couldn't remember ever seeing a man like this—not face to face, anyway. It suddenly felt as though there was an elephant sitting on her chest.

"How can you go home if you don't know where home is?" he asked evenly.

He had a point there and she managed to drag her gaze away from his beautiful torso to look into his eyes and try to deal with it.

"You don't understand," she said. "I don't belong here. I'm not comfortable. I need to leave."

"You need to stay." He grimaced and tried to soften his tone a bit. "You can't get out, anyway. The moment you open a door or a window, alarms will go off and sirens will sound and the dogs will be released. You wouldn't get two steps out of the house before the guards and dogs would bring you down." He looked at her narrowly. "And they play rough. This is serious business, Marisa."

She didn't waver. "You could call them off."

He sighed. "So you could go wander the streets of the city? Be serious. We've just overthrown a vicious regime and there are still plenty of their supporters around. There are murders in the streets every night. No one on either side is willing to give anyone the benefit of the doubt." He shrugged his wide shoulders. "It's a cold, cruel world. You're better off here."

"That's your opinion."

He stared down at her without speaking for a long moment.

His silence was making her jumpy. "You really have no right to stop me, you know," she added stoutly.

"You think not?" he said softly, moving closer. "You haven't been paying attention, Marisa. I have every right."

She blinked up at him. He was so close she caught a hint of the liquor he'd been drinking. Against all reason, it smelled sweet and enticing. She had to fight back the urge to lean toward him. Funny how his physical presence drew her in even while his inflexible words put her back up.

"Because you're a prince? Are you giving me some sort of…of royal order?"

His mouth twisted and his eyes glittered. "Exactly."

"Oh really!" She tried to glare. "I didn't realize restoration of the royal family was going to change all our lives in quite such a personal way."

"Get used to it," he said, speaking very softly again. "It's for your own good."

His tone was making her very nervous and the way his gaze kept dropping to her mouth was causing butterflies in her stomach. There was a pulse between them, a rhythmic sensuality that was getting as obvious as jungle drums. He was going to kiss her, wasn't he? All the signs were there. And that was no good at all. She had to get away from him before that happened.

She licked her lips, trying to think of a killer phrase or bit of logic, something that would permanently win this argument and let her turn on her heel and stomp off. But it was too late. As she stood there, transfixed, he moved even closer and his hand went to her hair, fingers spiking in until he'd cupped the back of her head in his palm and her will had turned to Jell-O.

He looked down into her face as though he

was struggling as hard to stay away as she was. This close, she could read the turmoil in his eyes, despite the darkness. Could he hear how hard her heart was beating?

She shook her head slightly, trying to pull away, but his hand tightened. She felt the warm sizzle of his breath on her face and then his mouth came down on hers and something magic happened. Her mind was screaming at her to get away, but her body wasn't listening to that anymore. She didn't resist at all. Instead, she sighed softly and curled herself into his embrace as though she'd been starved for male affection for a long, long time and needed this in order to survive.

He pulled her up against the length of his solid body. She put a hand up to stop him, but it landed on his exquisite chest and she flattened it against a rounded mound of the hardest muscles she'd ever touched. She couldn't think anymore. She could only feel. And what she felt was hypnotic and wonderful.

His mouth was hot and hard and sensual in a way she'd never known before. He tasted so good—but then, temptation always tasted good, didn't it?

When he pulled back, she found herself yearning toward him, as though she couldn't stand to lose his heat. Slowly, he disentangled their limbs until she was standing all alone again.

"I shouldn't have done that," he said gruffly, holding her off.

Looking up at him, she couldn't speak. She'd never been kissed quite like that before, and she wasn't sure how to react. Her gaze went to his mouth and she tried to say something, but no words came.

He made a sound of pure disgust, startling her until she realized he was responding to his own actions, not hers.

"Marisa," he said, looking away and raking his fingers through his own hair, "if you must go, of course, you must go. But not now. Not in the middle of the night. The city isn't safe."

Huh? Oh. That again. She'd almost forgotten. They'd been arguing about her desire to leave. Somehow it had slipped her mind. Good thing he'd reminded her. Taking a deep breath, she wished she could go back to the fray, but her thought processes didn't seem to be working very well. Did kissing a prince tend to turn your brain to cotton candy? Maybe so. At any rate, she was feeling warm and fuzzy and all the fight she'd been so full of had oozed away.

"Go back to your room," he said shortly, looking back at her as though it was a painful thing to do. "You can go in the morning. I won't stop you."

Picking up his glass, he turned and left the room. And Marisa found herself moving like a zombie, but doing exactly what he'd told her to do.

Marisa stretched and yawned and looked about the room. Someone had pulled back the heavy drapes and sunlight was streaming in, catching on the rich embroidery of the bed covers and the elaborate flocking on the wallpaper. The room was enchanting. She knew she'd never had such a beautiful place of her own before and she smiled, enjoying it for a moment. She'd slept well and she felt good. She was going to let her mind slowly drift into full awareness, and surely she would remember all those things that had been hiding from her since last night. Her name was Marisa and she'd come to the city from a town called…

She waited expectantly. Nothing happened.

Okay, just relax. It was going to come to her. *Just drift and try to picture it.*

Still nothing.

Oh come on! This was so darn frustrating! Why couldn't she remember? It was right there, just out of reach.

Maybe…maybe something else was getting in the way. Maybe if she just let herself think about it for a moment, let the memory of the prince and his touch and his taste…

No! A spasm of pure reaction made her stretch out and then curl up again. She couldn't go there. Thoughts like that made her stomach fall, like riding on a roller coaster. It was too dangerous.

She'd been kissed by a prince. That was not a good thing. The chorus from that nursery-rhyme tune wafted into her brain again. *Oh what a lucky girl, to be the prince's plaything.*

"Not in this lifetime," she promised her reflection in the big mirror on the other side of the room. No, she wasn't going to let the prince's kiss corrupt her thinking. She had enough common sense in her soul to fight it. At least, she hoped she did.

"I'm getting out of here," she told herself out loud and with determination. "I'm going to leave the palace and hunt down my suitcase and once I have that, I'll be able to figure out what is going on. I don't need a royal intervention."

"Nobody expects a royal intervention," said a teasing voice that just barely preceded Princess Carla appearing through the doorway. She smiled at Marisa, blue eyes dancing.

"Good morning, my dear. I hope you won't begrudge me a morning visit, no intervention implied."

Marisa laughed. "You caught me talking to myself. I feel foolish."

"Don't." Carla plopped down on the side of the

bed. "We all need to give ourselves a good talking to now and then. So, tell me, have you remembered anything?"

Marisa shook her head. "Not really. It's so odd. I feel fine and nothing is really wrong. I remember myself as a person, but not the specifics of how I got here. Does that make any sense?"

"No." Carla laughed. "But I think I know what you mean." She took Marisa's hand and looked earnestly into her face. "And you don't remember who the father of the baby is?"

"No. Not at all." Marisa hesitated. She had the urge to go on, to unburden herself to this friendly princess—she seemed so open and welcoming. But she knew it would be wise to be a little discreet. Some deep instinct was warning her that spilling her guts just might get her into big trouble.

"For some reason," she went on carefully, "the father of the baby doesn't loom large in my desire to know the truth. It seems almost irrelevant. It makes me think he hasn't been a factor in my life for quite some time."

Carla nodded. "You don't have the traditional rings," she reminded her. "So it doesn't seem you would be married."

Marisa nodded.

"Well, I think we should call in a specialist. Dr. Zavier is all very well, but what does he know about these things? Tell you the truth, he's always been our family doctor but I've never cared for him much. We really need to get some expert advice on what to do with you."

Marisa smiled at her intensity. "I appreciate all you and your brother are doing, but this really isn't your problem, you know."

"Sure it is." Carla grinned. "We like you." She waved a careless hand in the air in a mock show of royal hubris. "And anyway, what else do I have to do today?"

That made Marisa curious. She'd never wondered much about what being a princess might be all about, but she would never have a better opportunity to find out.

"Carla, what do you do with your time?" she asked her.

"Me? Oh, I'm quite busy. I do good works."

Marisa wrinkled her nose. "What sort of good works?"

Carla made a face. "Oh, I don't know. I have a list of them somewhere. I'll find it and get back to you." They laughed at each other again. "To tell you the truth, I haven't really begun yet. From what I understand, representatives of different charity groups and other organizations come to me and I go speak to them at their luncheons. Help them with fundraising. Cut the ribbon at openings. Hit ships with bottles. Things like that." She shrugged. "At least, that's what I'm told. Isn't that what princesses do?"

Marisa frowned. "I thought they partied with the jet-set crowd."

Carla leaned forward conspiratorially. "You know, I thought that too. But so far…" She looked back over her shoulder to make sure they weren't being overheard. "My brothers are pretty protective. We grew up in exile, you know. It was very different for us. Over the last few years, with the war and my mother passing away and now my father too, we haven't really had much partying in our lives. But I'm looking forward to giving it a try."

Marisa smiled at the younger woman, thinking she was glad to have her for a friend—for the moment at least. Reaching out, she gave her a hug. "Be careful out there, Carla. No wild affairs with rock stars. That doesn't do anyone any good."

"Oh no, of course not!" She blushed prettily. Sliding off the high bed, she started toward the door. "Come on downstairs, sleepyhead," she said. "The morning room is laid out with plenty of things for breakfast. I'm going to go ahead and eat now, because I have a gown fitting in half an hour. But you can eat any time you choose. See you later."

Marisa hesitated. It was on the tip of her tongue to say again, "But I have to leave." She knew she was getting to be a one-note samba on that score, so she held her tongue. But before Carla got completely away, she took a deep breath and asked the question that had been bothering her since her midnight encounter with the prince.

"Carla, who is Andrea?"

Carla spun around and stared at her. "Where did you hear that name?"

"Your brother. I startled him and he called me Andrea."

Carla's gaze was troubled. "I don't know why he would have done that," she said shortly. "She's dead."

Turning back toward the door, she walked away with a determined step. Marisa's breath caught in her throat. No wonder he'd seemed so haunted last night. If he'd actually thought she was someone he'd loved and lost, even for a moment, that must have cut like a knife. She sighed. She really did have to leave this place. Everything was way too complicated for her.

"I suppose I just wasn't meant for the royal life," she muttered to herself as she slid out of bed and padded to the bathroom.

CHAPTER FIVE

PRINCE Nico was on the terrace that flared out over the estate from his bedroom suite. From where he sat, he could see the gardens and the small forest beyond them. To the right were the ancient Gothic buildings that housed certain agencies of the government. To the left was the entry yard, the guard building, the gate to the rest of his country and all its citizens. He could feel them out there, just waiting for things to get better. He only hoped they would be patient a little longer. He felt like a man sitting on a powder keg. If he and his brothers didn't get off the dime soon, the whole thing would blow up in their faces.

But he wasn't really thinking much about that today. Today, sitting at a wrought-iron table, he was having coffee and reading the morning paper.

At any rate, he was trying to read it. He stared at the headlines, but all he could think about was Marisa. What was he going to do with her? The new government was not yet able to use DNA or fingerprints or any other sort of identity confirmation. All records had been destroyed in the war. Unless she regained her memory, or someone turned up who knew who she was, there wasn't much hope of identifying her and he was going to have to find a way to care for her without getting involved himself.

Of course, she had every right to walk out of the palace and never look back. He knew that. But he wanted to avoid that at all costs. She and her baby needed protection.

At the same time, he knew he couldn't keep her here. It was perfectly obvious he wouldn't be able to keep his hands off her if she was around all the time. Quickly, he mused over various options as they presented themselves to him and soon he thought he had a pretty good idea.

Chauncy appeared with a glass of orange juice and the morning mail. He looked up at the man who had served his family for so many years.

"Ah, Chauncy. I'm glad you're here. I need you to make some arrangements for me."

"Of course, Your Highness."

He outlined a plan to have teams sent out to try to find Marisa's suitcase as the first order of business, then got down to the matter at hand.

"What I have in mind is some sort of an old-fashioned boarding house, a nice place, well-decorated, with private rooms off a central living room and dining facilities."

Chauncy went very still and his brow showed the tiniest of frowns. "Might I ask what such a place would be for?"

"You may indeed. I'd like it to be a home for nice women, especially women who may have babies on the way and need a place to stay. There should be a sort of den-mother person hired to make sure everything runs smoothly." He frowned, thinking. "A cook, I suppose, a house-keeper, a gardener and that sort of thing. You can handle the details, I'm sure."

Chauncy coughed discreetly.

Nico looked up at him questioningly. "Yes?"

"Your Highness, I'm sure you have some specific young ladies in mind. Perhaps if you filled me in on just what your plans are…"

Nico's brow lowered appreciably. He would have preferred to keep things on a theoretical basis, but he realized that was unrealistic. Surely Chauncy already guessed the truth, so what was he waiting for?

"It's for her, of course," he said shortly. "Marisa. She needs a place to stay. She also needs consistent medical care, actually, but she will resist that." He nodded as he thought that over. "This way we can keep an eye on her and provide for things like a decent diet and doctors' visits and such without worrying that she's in any sort of jeopardy."

Chauncy looked stricken and tried to hide it. "Might I suggest that, pure as your motives obviously are—if the tabloids got hold of this they wouldn't see it that way."

"Hmm?" Nico looked up at the older man. A look of surprise flashed over his face.

"Oh my God. You're right." He laughed humorlessly. "What was I thinking? They would assume I was setting up a comfortable bordello for myself, wouldn't they?"

"I'm afraid so, Your Highness."

The prince sighed and threw down his pen. "Okay, back to the drawing board," he muttered. "I'll have to think of something else."

"I have a suggestion, Your Highness."

"Yes?"

"I know of a residence hotel for young women who come to the city looking for work. It's clean and well-run. I happen to know there is an opening right now."

Nico frowned, considering. "Do you vouch for the place?"

"I do, sir. My sister runs it."

Nico's eyes widened. "Your sister? When did you get a sister?"

"I've always had one, sir."

Nico stared at him. He'd known this man all his life. More than a servant, Chauncy had often seemed to be his father's best friend. He winced now, missing his father and the wise counsel he so often gave. Having Chauncy as backup was invaluable. He loved the man. Why hadn't he known he had a sister? But that was neither here nor there at the moment.

"Well, that might be the answer to the problem. How soon do you think she could move in?"

"I'll be happy to take her over this morning, Your Highness."

"Oh. That soon?" Nico swore at himself the moment the words were out of his mouth. The sooner the better. Wasn't that the whole point? It would be best if he knew she was well taken care of but he never had to see her again. And he could get on with his life.

"Very well. That might just fit the bill. And in the meantime, don't forget to start the great suitcase search immediately. Thank you, Chauncy."

Chauncy bowed his way off the terrace but Nico hardly noticed. Now that he'd taken care of that little problem, he should be able to rest easy. Instead there was a restless anger smoldering inside him. Rising to go inside, he cracked his knee on the wrought-iron table and cursed harshly, barely resisting the urge to throw the damn thing over the railing.

Oh yes, he could tell this was going to be a great day. Still muttering curses, he limped off to change into other clothes. He was headed for the palace gym. If there was one thing he needed, it was a good, exhausting workout.

Marisa searched through the garments in the wardrobe and picked out a cute yellow sundress. She never wore things like this—at least, she didn't think she did. Still, somehow she was attracted to it today. But it had been raining the night before. Was a dress like this going to be appropriate? She went to the window to look out and judge the weather.

The rain had cleaned the city and the sun was giving it a special shine. Everything looked warm and inviting. There was a lovely view from her vantage point. The window faced the front of the palace and she could see out past the iron fence, past the barricades left from the war, into the surrounding neighborhood with its wealthy homes.

And as she was looking over the handsome estates across the street from the palace, she also saw, just out of the corner of her field of vision, someone slip behind a stone wall and duck down, out of sight. Funny. She stared at the place where she'd seen it happen for a long moment, but there was no movement. Still, she was sure she'd seen someone go into hiding. She couldn't think why anyone would be keeping watch on the palace and trying to hide that fact, but there was something ominous about it. She made a mental note to tell the prince what she'd seen, shrugged and turned back to dressing.

Everything had looked warm and sunny outside, so she put on the dress without a qualm. Looking in the mirror, she liked what she saw. Her belly protruded a bit, but the bloused waist hid most of that. She looked pretty good, if she did say so herself. Looking around the room, she wanted to hug herself. This was all so nice.

Whoa there, she told herself quickly. There

was no point in growing to like this lifestyle too much. By noon, she should be out of here, but for now, she made her way downstairs and for the first time, took a really good look around.

What she saw staggered her. The place was a palace, for heaven's sake! The floors were marvelously inlaid with marble and other luminous stone, highlighted here and there by large sumptuous Persian rugs. The walls were richly textured with velvet-like coverings and huge ancestral paintings hung on every wall. The furniture was large, mostly heavy and reeking of age and quality, with fancy carvings and gilded decoration. It was enough to make her feel very small and ordinary. She tried to imagine what it must have been like for a young girl to come here straight from the countryside to work as a maid. Terrifying!

She wandered for a few minutes, awestruck, then found herself staring at the morning room where, rumor had it, breakfast was to be found. An older man and a middle-aged woman were just leaving. They looked startled to see her, but both nodded, glanced at each other, and left the scene as she nodded back.

"Probably wondering if I'm actually one of those new employees who's lost her way," she muttered. But never mind. Here she was, alone with piles of wonderful food.

There was a table set for breakfast, but she didn't want to stay and risk ending up eating with the prince. Very quickly, she filled her plate with bakery items and chunks of fruit, then grabbed a steaming cup of coffee before trying the French doors to the garden outside. One opened at her touch and she was outside, heading for the small forest of fluttering trees she could see on the other side of the garden pond. Balancing her cup and her plate, she walked fast, hoping to get into the shelter of the trees before she was seen.

A few more steps and she was home free, following a well-worn path that soon led her to a bubbling brook snaking its way through the woods. Putting her cup and plate of food down on a large, flat rock, she wandered down to the stream's edge, enjoying the cool, clear water.

What a place this was! It was like being in the middle of an ancient forest in the center of a bustling city. Looking up at the sky beyond the treetops, you wouldn't even know a busy population was rushing about only a couple of blocks away. The music of the brook masked any traffic noise from just beyond the fence, but she could hear the sound of the breeze rustling the leaves and the cheerful chirping of birds in the trees… and the sound of someone on a cell phone, coming her way down the forest path.

"Oh bother," she cried softly, knowing right away it was going to be the prince. Yes, she could hear that it was his voice. She couldn't run into him alone again, like last night. Looking around quickly, she searched for some place to hide. There was a little brush-covered island accessed by strategically placed logs. Without giving it a second thought, she bounded across the stream, stepping on one log then another and vaulting her way into the brushy area.

Unfortunately, the bush turned out to be a lot more threadbare than it had looked from the

banks. She crouched down anyway, knowing
that she wasn't well hidden at all and praying he
would be too involved in his conversation to
notice her there.

He came into view and it looked as though she
might be in luck. He was arguing with someone,
speaking sharply, and he passed through the little
glen without a glance her way.

Obviously dressed for a workout, he looked
very different from when she'd seen him before.
Shiny black compression shorts hugged his
muscular upper thighs like a second skin and
his loose-fitting tank top revealed a pair of very
strong shoulders and the gorgeous bulge of some
extremely fine biceps. She gulped. Every time
she saw the man, he just looked better.

Just as he was about to pass by completely, he
stopped short, looked back, and did a double
take at her breakfast, neatly set out on the flat
rock. He cocked that majestic eyebrow, then
broke off his conversation and closed his phone,
tucking it into a pocket as he turned back in her
direction.

"Marisa, come on out, I can see you," he said, looking mystified. "And anyway, you left your plate of goodies behind." He shook his head as she rose from the bush, her cheeks hot. "What the hell are you hiding for?"

Despite the fact that her embarrassment was only too obvious and visible, she held her chin high and pretended to have a scrap or two of dignity still left.

"One would think, being royal and all, that you would have better manners," she said, clinging to the theory that a good offense was the best defense.

"Manners?" He stared at her, completely out to sea.

"Yes." She cast a careless gesture into the air with her hand. "Seeing a lady in distress at being found in the forest, a real gentleman would walk on by, pretending he hadn't seen a thing."

He shook his head as though he really didn't know what to make of her and had given up trying.

"A real lady wouldn't be hiding in the bushes in the first place," he noted sensibly. "Anyway, what if you were stuck there? Caught by a bramble or with a sprained ankle or something. Being a real gentleman, it would be my duty to come to your rescue."

She gaped at his presumption. "I can rescue myself very well, thank you."

"Can you?" He was relaxing into amusement and he gave her a half grin that sent her pulse spinning, but it didn't last more than a few seconds.

"Come on," he said, growing somewhat impatient. "Take my hand." He offered it to help her back across the logs.

"I can do it myself," she said dismissively. "I got here on my own. I can get back." But she stared at the first log thinking, *How the heck did I get here, anyway?* It suddenly looked like a long leap. One misstep and she would be in the water. She hesitated, trying to decide where to plant her foot.

"Give me your hand," he ordered, leaning out as far as he could without landing in the water himself. "Give me your hand or I'm going to come over there and pick you up and carry you across."

She looked up into his eyes. He meant it. Her

heart began to thump against her chest at the thought. She put her hand out and he took it in his and guided her back across the logs with no problem at all.

And once he had her safely on the bank, he released her hand and stepped away from her. Obviously he was as anxious to avoid a repeat of what had happened the night before as she was. That should have been a relief, but somehow it was an annoyance at the same time.

Their gazes met and held for a second or two, but it was so obvious they were both thinking about the midnight kiss, they quickly disengaged.

"How are you feeling?" he asked her. "Did you sleep well last night?"

"Yes, actually. I slept very well."

She glanced at him sideways. His stance was wide and balanced like an athlete. She had to admit he had better legs than most men. From all evidence, he had better almost everything than most men. In fact, he was a prince a girl could dream about. As long as she remembered it was all fantasy anyway.

"Any change in your memory problem?" he asked.

She shook her head. "No."

He didn't say anything more. She knew he was looking at her in her yellow dress. She wished she had the nerve to look into his eyes and try to judge what he was thinking. Did he like what he saw?

Marisa! Don't go there!

Swallowing hard, she looked up at him and he looked into her eyes and then both gazes skittered quickly away again.

"Have you talked to Chauncy?" he asked, kicking at a stone with his foot.

"No." It seemed an odd question. She turned his way but pinned her gaze to a woodpecker in the tree behind him. "Why?"

He cleared his throat, then said quickly, "He and I have devised a plan for you."

That set off warning bells all through her system. How dare he? Now she could look him fully in the face.

"Oh really?" she said, trying to remain calm. "I don't suppose it might have occurred to you to consult me? Or even that I might have plans for myself?"

He frowned. "You don't understand...."

"Oh, I think I do."

She took a deep breath and counted to three. There was no point in getting hysterical. She'd already made a spectacle of herself by attempting to hide in a bush.

Nice and easy, that was the ticket. Another deep breath. *Okay*.

Looking into his blue eyes, she tried to look as earnest as she felt. "Seriously, I appreciate all you've done for me, but I need to be on my own. As soon as I finish my breakfast…"

"Breakfast!" He turned to look at her plate of delicious-looking pastries. "Is that what you call it? What is that stuff you're eating?"

She blinked, not sure what he was complaining about.

"Carla told me to go ahead and take anything I wanted from the spread in the morning room. I'm sorry if…"

"No, you're welcome to the food, it's just your

selections I have issues with." He scowled at her. "Are you still having a hard time remembering that you're pregnant?"

She flushed. So that was the crux of the problem. She should have known. "No, not at all. I'm aware of it every minute. This baby means everything to me."

"Really? Then where's your glass of milk? Why aren't you eating eggs? Or maybe a little oatmeal."

"I've got fruit. Look." She pointed out a nice red strawberry sitting proudly on the plate next to a piece of sugar-encrusted pastry, dabbed with whipped cream.

"Have you had any nutritional counseling at all?" he demanded.

She rolled her eyes at him. "Well, if I knew that, I'd be remembering things, wouldn't I?" Her gaze sharpened. "What do you know about nutritional counseling for pregnant women?"

The flash of some emotion she couldn't identify told her she'd said something it would have been better not to say. She took a step backwards, a quiver of unease shivering down her spine. But before he got a response out, his cell phone rang. Swearing softly, he pulled it out, looked at the caller ID and gave her a quick nod.

"I've got to take this call," he said shortly. "I'm sure you can find your way back to the palace by yourself."

"Of course." She gave him a look of manufactured disgust. "I can see it from here."

He hesitated. "If I don't see you again before you go, I just want to say…"

It was evident he couldn't say what he really wanted to. She blinked at him, waiting.

"It's been very nice having you stay with us," he said stiffly at last, making it sound like a rote pleasantry that meant nothing. "Good luck to you in the future."

He turned away quickly, not waiting for an answer. She bit her lip as she watched him walk on into the depths of the tiny forest, cell phone to his ear. The worst part was, she knew very well she was overwhelmed with disappointment to see him leave.

"And that only proves that I'm late for the

leaving myself," she muttered as she collected her pastries and headed back toward the palace.

She had no idea what he'd been talking about but his attitude seemed to show that he also realized she had to go. In fact, he was pretty much saying goodbye, wasn't he?

Perfect. She was as good as gone.

A half hour later, Prince Nico had showered and was dressing for a meeting with the prime minister. He had a lot of complaints about things the PM was doing and he needed to marshal his arguments. He should have been thinking up strategies. Instead, he was mooning over a woman. And he couldn't seem to stop.

At first he'd told himself it was because she was pregnant, but since he'd kissed her, he knew better. Against all logic, he wanted her badly— so badly his insides were churning with a deep, hungry restlessness that was making him feel like a caged beast.

"But don't worry," he muttered darkly to his

reflection as he finished using his electric shaver for a little touch up. "I'm not going to do anything about it."

At any rate, soon this all would be moot. Chauncy should be getting her packed up at this very moment. By the time he got back from meeting with the PM, she would be gone, and he would never see her again.

Ouch. He didn't know why that made him feel sick to his stomach. He should be happy. He should be celebrating.

"Whoopie," he muttered, looking through his ties for a good one. Celebrating was the last thing he felt like doing. He wished he could go back to the gym and put his body through another torture routine. Anything to get his mind off Marisa.

Instead, he went out restlessly onto the terrace and leaned on the railing. And there she was, walking on a path through the rose garden, still in the yellow sundress. He knew he should go back in and ignore her, but he couldn't. This might be the last time he ever saw her. She seemed to dance along the walkway, making an enchanting picture with her light-blond mass of curls catching the sunlight and floating around her face like a halo, her long, lovely legs, her rounded breasts, her pretty face, her slender arms with the hands fluttering like elegant birds. For the rest of his life he would have that picture and all he would have to do was close his eyes and dredge up the memory of her in that yellow sundress and he'd be happy.

Happy? He slapped himself in the forehead. Was he nuts? She didn't make him happy now, so why would memories do it?

He watched as she headed into the house through the French doors. There was no getting around it, she could surely brighten a life. Not his, of course. But somebody's.

He turned back into his room and felt like kicking something. But he had no time for that. The prime minister was waiting.

He was almost finished creating the perfect knot in his tie when Carla came barging into his room, waving a set of papers.

"Bad news," she cried, her cheeks bright red and her eyes sparkling with anger. "Look at these," she added, thrusting the papers at him. "The wash maid found them concealed in Marisa's clothes."

He looked at them curiously as she spread them out on his dresser where he could get a better view. The papers had the patina of ancient parchment. Each was covered with ink forming odd symbols, the like of which he'd never seen before. Stained and tattered, they looked like something that might have turned up in a treasure chest dug up in some excavation site. He reached out and touched one of them gingerly, afraid it might crumble. The symbols meant nothing to him.

"What do you mean they were concealed in her clothes?" he asked, fingering the paper and frowning.

"In the linings. Part of the stitching had come loose and the maid pulled these out. Can you believe this? The whole amnesia thing is obviously a hoax."

His head came up and he stared at her levelly. "What are you talking about?"

She nodded wisely. "It looks like your little bird is a lousy opposition spy after all."

CHAPTER SIX

PRINCE Nico stared at his sister Carla.

"You think Marisa is a spy?" he asked skeptically. "What evidence do you have of that?"

"Just look at these!" she cried, waving a hand at the papers. "We've caught her red-handed."

"I don't get it," he said, shaking his head. "How does this prove she's a spy?"

She looked as though she thought he was being willfully obstinate. "What are you talking about? She came here pretending to be a lost soul with amnesia, and yet now we find secret papers hidden in her clothes, papers written in code. It's pretty obvious she's up to no good, isn't it? Chauncy thinks so."

"Has he seen these?"

"Yes. Chauncy was with me. He has no doubt

she's a spy. We swore the maid to secrecy, but it's bound to get out." She gave her brother a challenging look. "What'll we do with her?"

Nico stared at the papers. This did look bad, but he couldn't quite join the posse yet. "You tell me, Carla. What do you think we should do?"

"Have her arrested, of course."

He gave her a pained look. "On what grounds?"

Carla shrugged dramatically. "She's carrying secret documents about."

"When did that become a crime?"

She blinked and looked rebellious. "You can declare it a crime, can't you? You're the care-taker prince while Dane is away."

He groaned. "Carla, we're trying to establish the rule of law in this country. Once any group starts making their own laws, you can throw out that brand-new constitution."

"There must be something you can do. It's just obvious she's trying to undermine our family. Can't you see that?" She looked thoughtful. "Maybe we should put her under questioning.

You know methods, don't you? From your time in the war?"

His face darkened. "Carla, if you understood what you're talking about, you wouldn't say such things."

"It's a new time, Nico. You're always telling me that. We have enemies everywhere. We have to take extreme measures to protect ourselves."

"Within the law." He turned from her, beginning to realize how serious this could be. He would stick to the law, of course, but what if more came out and the law said he had to hand Marisa over to the authorities? Everything in him rebelled at the thought. He just couldn't believe she could be spying here.

And yet, what had she been doing skulking about in the woods, hiding from him? Had she hoped to overhear his phone conversations? He tried to remember who he'd been talking to. The Greek ambassador. Nothing particularly classified there. But maybe she was waiting to hear whomever he might be calling next. Who knew? And if she was spying, whom was she spying for?

Shaking that thought away, he picked up the phone to call the butler. "Chauncy, cancel my meeting with Grieg. Tell him I'll call him later. And get Trendyce over here. I need to talk to our Intelligence Coordinator."

"Immediately, Your Highness," the butler responded. "And as to that other matter, the transfer of the young lady to my sister's residence hotel?"

Looking into his wide mirror, Nico noted the haggard look in his own face. "We'll have to put that on hold for now. But keep it in abeyance. We may be making use of your sister's hotel soon enough. We'll have to see how this pans out."

"As you wish, Your Highness."

Carla flopped down on his bed and watched as he talked and then closed his phone. "What are you going to do?"

He glanced back at where she sat, looking young and naive, as usual. "I'm going to have Trendyce take these papers and find out what the hell is going on."

"Good. And the police?"

He turned to look at her. "Carla…"

"She needs to cool her heels in a jail cell for awhile," his young sister said stoutly. "I've just been reading a history of England. Opposition spies were always being arrested in the old days."

Nico shook his head decisively. "No, no jail cell. The woman is pregnant, Carla."

"Are you kidding? What if that's phony, too? What if this whole thing is a ruse to play on your sympathies and wheedle her way into your good graces?"

"Dr. Zavier confirmed the pregnancy." Nico frowned. "And anyway how does that track with her desire to leave?"

Carla made a sound of deprecation. "That's just another ploy to get your sympathy."

"You think so?"

"Of course it is." Carla dangled her legs over the side of the bed. "I say she goes to the tower."

He swung around to stare at her. "Carla, we don't have a tower."

"Yes we do. The prison at Elmgore."

He shook his head, looking at her incredulously, wondering if the family hadn't protected her from real life for much too long. "You can't call that a tower. And this isn't medieval England."

She stuck her nose into the air. "It ought to be."

He stared at her again. A part of him wanted to laugh, but this situation was far from amusing. A very painful knot was developing deep inside him and he knew it was only going to get worse.

Marisa knew something was wrong. The sweet, friendly and funny Carla of midnight and morning had transformed into a tight-lipped young woman with a cool gaze now that it was almost noon. What had happened?

Was it because she was balking at the plan Nico and Chauncy had cooked up to put her out of the way and into a residence hotel on the other side of town? She didn't blame them, really. If she'd been in their shoes, she might have thought it was a good idea. After all, it got her out of their hair but under supervision, so no one could claim they'd abandoned her to the winds of fate. Good for them.

But bad for her. She had no intention of being managed. She wanted to get out in the mix and start looking for her suitcase—and her place in the world. Surely it would come back to her as she walked around the city. Wouldn't it?

So when Chauncy had told her what the plan was, she'd very politely told him she thought it stunk. And she wanted to talk to the prince about just how badly.

Chauncy had tried to dissuade her, telling her Nico was busy and was off to see the prime minister and other things to put her off. But she was having none of it. She was leaving all right, but not before she told Nico just what she thought of his plan.

It had been shortly after that awkward confrontation that everyone had begun treating her as though she'd developed a communicable disease. But really, Carla's attitude was the one that puzzled her the most. Carla had been such a darling and now she acted as though they were enemies. It was disappointing, and truth to tell, it rather hurt her feelings.

Never mind. She was leaving. But she had to see the prince before she went. So she was wandering through the house, trying to figure out where his room was, and suddenly she came face to face with him on the stairs.

"Marisa," he said, stopping on a step above her.

"Prince Nico," she replied, searching his face to see if he had turned on her, too.

"I was just coming to look for you."

"That doesn't surprise me," she said, meeting his gaze and holding it. "I want to know what's happened. What's wrong?"

His eyes darkened with what looked to her like suspicion. That stung. He was dressed for business and obviously ready to go out. Now he looked like her picture of a prince again, cool, detached, superior. There was no way a man like this would have kissed her.

"What are you talking about?" he asked softly.

"All of a sudden people are looking at me as though I'm the…the enemy." All her bravado evaporated. "Please tell me. I know there's something. What happened?"

He nodded slowly, his gaze distant. "Very perceptive of you, Marisa," he said coolly. "Come with me. I'll show you what happened."

He continued down the stairs and she followed, heart beating harder and harder as her anxiety grew. Now she was really getting scared. After all, she didn't know a thing about herself. What if they had found out something very bad? What if she'd committed a crime? Or really was allied with their enemies? How could she defend herself or protect herself when she just didn't know?

He led her into the library where he swept the miscellaneous books and papers off the table onto the floor and put down a folder instead. Opening the folder, he took out three pieces of faded paper and spread them out on the table.

"These are what happened," he said, standing back so she could see them.

She leaned over them. They seemed to be ancient documents covered with odd symbols. For just a moment, something about them struck a bell. She looked harder. Could she be remembering something? But no, nothing else flickered in her memory banks. She turned back and looked at Nico.

"What are these?"

He studied her for a moment before answering. "You don't recognize them?"

"No. Should I?"

He searched her eyes for a bit longer, then shrugged. "They were sewn into the lining of your skirt."

"They were…" She looked puzzled as she figured this out, then gasped. "What right do you have to snoop into my clothes?"

"Your clothes were in my house being laundered by my laundry maid," he said, his voice rough as gravel. "I reserve the right to check for evidence of spying."

"Spying!" Her heart fell.

"That's what we're talking about."

Spying. Oh my.

"Funny," she said nervously, trying to joke. "And here I thought you were going to accuse me of stealing the silverware."

"Marisa, this could be disastrous. Be serious."

She was. She'd just been vamping, hoping for a sudden burst of insight to help her along. She had no idea what these pages of odd symbols represented, but there was no denying, it looked bad. She stared at them for another moment or two, trying to force memory. But nothing came. Disappointment almost choked her. This couldn't go on this way. Eventually, something had to give. Didn't it?

She shook her head, looking at him with all the veracity she could muster. Would he believe her? Why should he? He didn't really know anything about her. And right now, she didn't know much about herself. But she was pretty darn sure she wasn't a spy.

"I'm telling you quite honestly, I don't know what these are."

"Never seen them before?"

She shook her head, her eyes filled with sadness. "Not that I remember."

His eyes narrowed as he watched her closely. "Ah yes, there is always that pesky memory thing at work here. Pretty convenient, isn't it?"

She was tempted to let anger rise in her voice, but she held it back. She was in big trouble and she knew it. "Believe me, if I could get rid of this…memory block or whatever it is, I would."

He stared down into her eyes for what seemed like forever, then turned away. "I've called in the intelligence services to decipher these symbols," he told her as he walked toward the window, hands shoved down into his pockets. "I'll talk to you again once they've made their report."

She assumed she was being dismissed. This was not going to be a good time to bring up her own questions, but she needed a few answers of her own. She made a quick exploration into his hard gaze and decided to chance it.

"About Chauncy and this plan you two cooked up," she began.

He swung around to face her straight-on. "Forget that," he said shortly. "Things have changed. You're staying here for the rest of the day. We'll decide what to do with you once we get this straightened out."

She knew better than to bring up her need to

leave again. "What are the options that are on the table?" she asked instead.

"That depends on the report," he responded.

She wanted to ask more. If she was a spy, was she considered a traitor? What kind of penalty did spies get these days? Should she be looking for ways to escape this place? That was pretty obvious. Too bad it didn't seem very possible.

She needed a champion in her corner, someone to lean on, someone on her side. The trouble was, the man who fit the bill was the very man accusing her.

By late afternoon Marisa was a nervous wreck. She'd spent hours in her room, waiting to be called down to hear the verdict. She couldn't read, she couldn't eat, she couldn't even think very straight. Was she a spy or wasn't she? And if she was, was she at all good at it? It hardly seemed likely.

The one positive sign was that she couldn't believe it. Sleuthing didn't seem to be a talent that came naturally to her. She just didn't seem to be the espionage type. As she tried to analyze it, she couldn't imagine that someone as bumbling and careless as herself—and as incompetent at hiding in bushes—could be a spy. Of course, maybe she was the sort of spy who sneaked around photocopying documents when no one was home instead of hiding out and overhearing conversations.

She sighed. No. Probably not.

A maid had brought her a nice lunch she hadn't touched, but other than that, she'd seen no one. There were books and magazines to read, and a television in the corner, but she couldn't keep her mind on anything but this accusation. It was so strange to be in agony and not know for sure what she was agonizing about. It was like shadow-boxing with a rival you couldn't really see. How could you possibly get anywhere? Or even know if you were making any progress?

Finally a rap came on her door.

"Marisa? I'm coming in."

Her heart leaped. It was Nico. She jumped up off the bed and looked around wildly, as though she needed to sweep something under the rug or hide evidence of wrongdoing. But there was nothing and no one. She'd changed into the stretchy running suit again, so she didn't even need to cover her knees. Feeling almost sullen, she sat back down on the bed and waited as he entered.

"Well?" she said, looking at him expectantly. "Am I a criminal or not?"

He stood looking at her for a long moment, hands loosely at his hips. His tie and suit coat were both gone and his crisp white shirt was open at the neck. Inanely, she wondered where he'd come by such a nice tan, then remembered that he seemed to make a habit of walking around the grounds in shorts and a tank top. That would do it.

"Our decoding crew has been working on it all afternoon and can't make heads nor tails of the symbols," he told her. "You wouldn't want to give them a clue, would you?"

She flashed a dark-eyed glare his way. "I told you, I don't know a thing about them."

"Yes, but they were sequestered in the lining

of your skirt. I'm afraid that means we're going to assign you custody of the entire issue until we get evidence otherwise."

She stared at him for a moment, then closed her eyes. "Of course," she said, sadness seeping into her voice. "In the meantime, I'm under house arrest for the duration. Isn't that the story?"

"Basically, yes."

She looked at him, feeling drained. She was tired of this, tired of being suspected, tired of not knowing enough about just what was involved to be able to fight it.

"Don't you see what a corner that puts me in? How can I make any progress in finding out who I am if I'm stuck here?" She sighed, fighting back tears. "I'm sure this isn't legal. The law must be on my side." She shook her head, searching for an idea. "Maybe I should talk to the police."

He grimaced. "Marisa, don't you understand? There are very few laws that are operative right now. Everything is in flux. Parliament is in turmoil trying to establish a new set of rules that will deal fairly and completely with all our people. But nothing has been established yet. In fact, right now, you have no recourse."

"I have no recourse at all?" Her eyes were huge with tragedy. "You can do whatever you want with me?"

If only it were that easy.

He almost grinned. It was hardly fair but he had to admit, the more upset she got, the more attractive he was finding her. Here he was staring down a woman who might be here as a viper in the bosom of his family, and all he could think about was how much he would like to kiss those cherry-pink lips again.

"As of right now, yes. There may be repercussions later, but I can risk that."

"Oh!" She closed her eyes and hugged herself, holding in the agony.

He felt a flash of sympathy for her and frowned hard to hide it before moving a step closer. "Marisa, do you understand why we're doing this?"

She turned her face away. "I understand that you're keeping me here against my will," she said stubbornly.

He sighed. She looked small and vulnerable sitting on her bed with her legs crossed in front of her. "I know you're unhappy. I know you feel you're being mistreated."

Moving closer, he dropped down to sit on the bed beside her. This was touchy. He was working hard at holding back his natural inclination—when in doubt, shout and force issues. That wouldn't work. Actually, it seldom did. But it was frustrating to know that, locked inside somewhere, she had the answers if only she knew how to find them. He was going to have to work hard to keep from doing anything that would just close her off. After all, he needed those answers.

And then it came to him—more than that, he didn't want her hurt. Something touched him as he looked at her. He thought it was probably because of Andrea that he felt so protective of Marisa.

Probably. Maybe.

"I've been wracking my brain trying to think of a way to explain this to you, Marisa. If you'll listen for a few minutes, I'll do my best to clarify it."

She met his gaze for only a second or two, nodded her compliance, and turned her gaze away again. Looking at her, he wasn't sure this was going to do any good, but he knew he had to try.

"Marisa," he began. "I don't know where you were during the war, or what side you were on. That's irrelevant now. But I want to go over a little history with you, just to clear things up."

He paused and she nodded again without looking at him.

"Since your memory of basic things that don't explicitly apply to you seems to be intact, you might remember that the rule of the House of Montenevada goes back over six hundred years. The only interruption has been over the last fifty years when the Acredonnas with their National Party had control. We spent the last five years fighting to get our patrimony back. Not because we felt some God-given right to rule, but because the Nationals were ruining the country and we have a responsibility to our people to protect them and take care of our heartland and its resources. And so the struggle began.

"Now that we've prevailed, we must fight hard to make this a decent country again. There are many forces arrayed against us. There's no guarantee that this is going to succeed. The Nationals are gathering strength in their enclaves. They are going to try to wrest power back away from us. We know that fight is coming. It's in this context that we have to be totally over the top in our security methods. *Have* to be. There is no alternative. If we let one thing go, that one little thing is bound to be the chink in our armor, the fatal flaw that can bring down the whole structure of our regime. We have to be more than careful. In fact, we sometimes have to be ridiculous."

She hadn't said anything for a long time and that seemed unusual. She was sitting with her head down, her mass of curly, lovely hair completely hiding her face. Reaching out, he broke the rule he'd set for himself that he wasn't going to touch her, and he pushed her hair back so he could see her eyes. They were brimming with tears.

"Marisa…"

She looked up at him as the tears began to make trails down her beautiful cheeks and her lower lip trembled with misery. "Oh Nico…"

His heart lurched.

"I just don't know," she admitted to him, sniffing helplessly, her heartbreak clear in her voice. "I can't even swear that I'm not one of them, because I just don't know."

He believed her. Everything in him believed her. If she was lying, if she was trying to pull one over on him, she was doing a wonderful job, because he was ready to do anything he could to help her right now. It was beyond his control. Before he knew what he was doing, he had her in his arms. And then there was no way to avoid kissing away her tears, murmuring sweet comfort and holding her close. She responded as though she was just as much a victim of this wave of emotion as he was.

He'd meant to calm her, to stop the tears and make her understand that he was on her side, that he wasn't going to jump to any conclusions, that he would do everything he could to make sure she got every benefit of the doubt.

But what started as simple comfort quickly became much more. He kissed her lips and when they opened, he just naturally entered her mouth and then his hands slid down her body and pulled her closer. She was softer than she looked, but with an underlying strength that warned him not to take her lightly. She was alive, vibrant, a force to be reckoned with. Her body felt so good, her skin so smooth, her kiss so hot. He felt an excitement he hadn't known for a long, long time.

She arched into his embrace, turning to take him against her and hold him tight. She was hungry for what he offered and she couldn't pretend otherwise. His own body tightened like a spring, coiled and ready, aching to plunge. She was soft and warm and smooth and he wanted every part of her to be his. He heard a deep sound and realized it was his own groan of a need to take her as his own.

Every part of him longed for her, agonizing to join her body with his. It felt like something that had to be, and yet he knew it was so wrong. Breathing raggedly, he pulled away from her, angry at himself, angry at fate, throbbing with the need to have her and wishing he could change that. He forced himself to breathe evenly, catching his breath, then looked at her, expecting frowns and recriminations.

Instead, she was smiling. "Oh!" she cried, as though something was startling her. Her hands went to her belly and she began to laugh.

"I feel it!" she said, eyes shining. "Oh Nico, I feel the baby."

Just like that, she'd forgotten what they'd just been doing. But he didn't blame her. He looked at where her hands were planted and suddenly he was smiling, too.

"Is this the first time?" he asked her.

"Yes. At least, this is the first time I'm sure it's

the baby. Oh, I feel as though I've been invaded by butterflies!" She laughed up at him, impulsively inviting him to share her joy. "Oh here, you try. Can you feel it?"

He couldn't feel a thing, but it didn't matter. As his palm cupped her belly, he felt as intimate as he'd ever felt with a woman. He and Andrea hadn't gotten to this stage. It was sad that Andrea had never felt their baby move. And yet, he was rather glad Marisa was traveling on to a level beyond what he'd experienced with the woman he loved. That seemed to make it more possible to appreciate her happiness without feeling a corresponding sense of pain for Andrea.

At least there was no doubt she was pregnant. And there was no doubt he was going to be involved with this woman in ways that were impossible to maintain. If he wanted to avoid that, he was going to have to do something quickly to stem this rapidly growing connection between them. He had to put a stop to it.

And he would. Very soon.

In the meantime, he had work to do. It was a

bit awkward pretending he hadn't just been kissing the hell out of her, but he managed to do it, telling her how things were going to be and preparing her for what was coming next.

"Marisa, I've had men scouring the city for your suitcase all day. So far, no luck. They did find this, however." Going to the door, he reached outside and he pulled in a large suede purse he'd left there and put it down in front of where she sat on the bed. "Do you recognize this?"

She frowned, looking inside, checking the pockets, unzipping the zippers, hoping to find something, anything, that would strike a chord. It was completely empty. Picking it up, she tried carrying it the way she assumed she usually carried her purse. She just wasn't sure.

"You know, it feels right." She looked up at him like a child, eager to please. "I like it. It might be mine." Then the clouds of anguish came back into her eyes. "Why can't I remember?"

Watching her, he didn't have a doubt in the world that she was telling the truth, as far as she was able to.

"I've got a memory expert flying in from Berlin tomorrow," he told her.

She looked stunned. "Just to see me?"

He smiled at her surprise. "Of course. Who else has amnesia around here?"

"Gee, I didn't realize I was so special."

She said it with a trace of bitterness, but there was a smile on her pretty face. He wanted to kiss her again, wanted to touch her, to make love to her for hours. But most of all he wanted to stay with her, and that meant he had to go.

He'd kissed her twice now. That was twice too many times and it couldn't happen again. He was going to have to find a way to keep his distance. That was the only way any of this could work.

CHAPTER SEVEN

"WE'RE going to keep her right here." Meeting with Carla in the library after talking to Marisa, Prince Nico was firm.

Carla reacted in surprise. "What? Here in the palace?"

"In the palace." He gazed levelly at his sister. "I will not have her in a prison."

"No prison?" Carla frowned. "But wait, Chauncy said his sister could…"

The prince held up his hand to stop her. "I'm telling you right now, Carla, that I don't think she's guilty. I've got Doctor Stein coming in from Berlin to examine her. Meanwhile, Intelligence says it may take weeks to break the code on those papers. I want her here for the duration. And that's the end of it."

Carla drew in a sharp breath. "Oh Nico. You haven't fallen for her, have you?"

His head reared back before he could stop himself. "No, of course not." Why was it that he didn't sound convincing, even to his own ears?

Obviously, Carla wasn't sold. "Are you crazy? What if she's married?"

He winced. Everything in him wanted to reject that possibility. If she was married and he was kissing her the way he'd been kissing her... No, that went against all his principles. It couldn't be. "I thought you agreed she wasn't married."

She shrugged and looked worried. "I thought the signs were good. But I don't know. She is pregnant, after all, so we know someone has been in her life. If it turns out she's married and you've let yourself fall in love with her..."

"I'm not in love with her," he said, exasperated. And he wasn't. Fascinated, yes. A bit smitten even. But not in love. He knew love. This wasn't it.

Carla was skeptical, but she held it back and pre-tended to believe him. "Good. Because, like they say, that crazy little thing called love can make you crazy. Or at the very least, break your heart."

He knew that. No one had to tell him about heartbreak, especially not his naive little sister. But he held his tongue. He didn't want to give her any more ammunition anyway.

Carla was shaking her head and staring at him as though she couldn't understand what had come over him. "Okay, so she won't go to prison, at least not yet. But I don't understand why she has to stay here. You don't really know anything about her. She's basically nothing but a stranger. Why do we have to keep her here?"

He turned from her. That was a question that was very hard to answer. He was tempted to say, "Because I want to," and leave it at that. But sometimes the truth just wasn't good enough, especially when Carla was prattling on and on about love. This wasn't really that. But for some reason, he couldn't stand to think of her away from his protection. He could protest that it was just the baby she was carrying until he was blue in the face, but he knew very well there was more to it than that. Still, it was no one's business. He was acting monarch while Dane was out of country. And he could do what he wanted to, damn it all!

"Tell me one thing." Carla frowned at him like an interrogator. "Is she really pregnant?"

"Carla, we've been over this before. Dr. Zavier is the final word on that."

She nodded, looking thoughtful. "I know, but if she's a spy, you have to question everything, don't you?"

He didn't answer and she went on.

"Well, how is this going to work?" Her eyes glittered with the possibilities. "Are you going to keep her locked in her room? Maybe put a guard on her?"

He half smiled at his sister's constant search for drama. "No, Carla. I'm going to put her in your custody."

"What?"

"Yes." He had to grin at her reaction. Shock was written across her face. But he was warming to the idea as he thought more about it. "She'll stay with us like a guest, only you'll be in charge of her safe-keeping. And she will be your companion."

Carla's mouth was open but no words came out. It seemed she was half appalled, half intrigued with the idea. "But…"

"Pretend you're both in the tower and you have the key."

"Oh." That captured her imagination right away. She thought for a moment, then beamed. "That might work."

Yes. It would work. For everyone but him. Because he was going to keep his distance, no matter how much he was tempted to get closer to Marisa. He was going to stay away. Maybe he would even find a reason to take a few business trips.

This was all nonsense anyway. He had more important things to think about. They had a country to build here. Love was for those who didn't have anything better to do. He was busy.

Marisa was trying to talk herself into going downstairs. She had no idea how she would be received, but it was time for the evening meal. She was just shoring up her determination to brave the possible enmity of the others when Carla appeared in her doorway.

"Hi," she said, her eyes big and soulful. "May I come in?"

"Of course." Marisa's smile was not as friendly as it might have been that morning, but if Carla was ready to make amends, she was ready to let bygones be bygones herself. She tensed, waiting to see how it was going to be.

Carla came all the way in, looked at Marisa and emitted a huge sigh that sent her shoulders drooping. "Nico sent me up here to ask you to join us for dinner."

Marisa's heart skipped a beat. He didn't have to send Carla. He could have sent a maid or Chauncy. Sending his sister was a good sign, wasn't it?

"Thank you," she said, and meant it.

Carla licked her lips and squared her shoulders. "And I want to apologize for being mean to you," she said, looking very contrite. "And I want to suggest we declare a truce until we learn what the truth is. Okay?" She looked hopeful.

"That would be great," Marisa said, amused at Carla's poses.

"Okay, good." Suddenly the younger girl looked happy again. "But I have to warn you," she added. "If it turns out you're really a spy, I'm going to hate you."

Marisa grinned. "If it turns out I'm really a spy, I'm going to hate myself," she told her.

Carla laughed and stepped forward impulsively to hug Marisa. By the time they were on the stairs, they were friends again and chattering like friends. Entering the huge, high-ceilinged dining room, Marisa looked around at the wonderful paintings that covered the walls—mostly seventeenth-century semi-nudes in the style of Rubens—and that might actually be the real thing for all she knew. The table was huge and set with sterling silver and crystal goblets that sparkled in the light from the heavy chandelier, but only one end was populated with about a dozen diners. She looked about quickly for the prince, but didn't see him.

A few older relatives were there, and the

couple she'd seen that morning at breakfast. She was introduced to a pair of young cousins from Belgrade who were staying at the palace while they attended classes at the newly reformed university. But as they took their seats, an elegantly attired middle-aged woman who was introduced to her as Lady Julia announced that Nico had been called away on business and wouldn't be joining them after all.

The sense of disappointment almost choked her. That set her back on her heels a bit, and made her color warmly. If she really cared this much, it was obviously time to back off. Sure he'd kissed her, but he was a prince and princes played around. It even said so in nursery rhymes. He was a prince and she was, for all she knew, a spy. There was no point in dreaming for things that were just downright impossible.

Gritting her teeth, she plastered on a smile and made small talk with the others at table. There was no way she was going to let anyone know that she wished the prince was there. No way at all.

* * *

Dr. Stein arrived the next morning. He spent an hour with her. Dr. Zavier had covered her physical vitals, so Dr. Stein concentrated on her emotional health, asking her questions that seemed far removed from the situation at hand. In the end, he told her to rest and to try to avoid stress. He thought she would recover her memory slowly over the next few weeks and promised to keep in touch to monitor her recovery. Other than that, he wasn't especially helpful, and she felt as if she had just wasted the time she'd spent with him.

She saw Nico a bit later in the morning, but only from a distance, and then he was gone again, heading for meetings with various members of the government. That was just as well, though it was funny how often she thought of things she wanted to talk to him about. For a man she hadn't even known two days before, he was certainly looming large in her consciousness. But that was probably because she didn't have much memory of anything that had happened before they met. Her mind had a big empty playground to fool around in and only Prince Nico as a toy.

She helped Carla cut flowers from the gardens for the huge bouquets that decorated all the public rooms of the house. She spent time in the little forest. She discovered a wonderful selection of historical volumes in the library, along with an exquisite collection of rare ancient cookbooks, which really drew her eye. By that afternoon she'd gotten to know most of the other residents of the palace a little better, including the people who had been at dinner the night before and other various relatives and old friends of the family.

There was Lady Julia of course, who acted as hostess for the royal family when they had banquets or balls, and as companion to Carla when she needed one. There was an uncle named Sergei, the Duke of Norgate, who seemed to be Nico and Carla's mother's brother. He was always wandering the halls, trying to get someone to come play chess with him. There were nieces and nephews and there was much talk about the fascinating Cousin Nadia whose clothes Marisa was wearing.

"Nadia lives close to the edge," Carla told her as they were sitting down for lunch. "Nico says she's always just one step away from a full-color spread in the tabloids." She smiled, her eyes glowing. "She's wonderful."

Nico entered the dining room in time to overhear what she'd said. His gaze met Marisa's and he nodded quickly, but responded to his sister's comment as he took his seat at the table.

"Our 'wonderful' cousin Nadia is a disaster waiting to happen. Like a snowball rolling downhill, she's gathering steam and scandal, which will eventually explode over all of us."

There was much nodding and a murmuring of agreement from the others at the table.

"She'll most likely ruin our reputation with the people," Uncle Sergei intoned dolefully. "It's bound to happen."

Marisa frowned. "Do you really think that whatever a madcap cousin of the family does is going to rebound on all of you?" she asked curiously.

"Oh yes," Lady Julia replied. "We've seen it happen before. The tabloids can take a one-day story and turn it into a month-long campaign against royalty in general."

It still seemed far-fetched to Marisa. "But I thought that was what royalty was for," she joked. "To get into scrapes that provide endless entertainment to the populace."

Talk about a lead balloon. The ones who didn't glare at her resentfully stared down at their plates and avoided her gaze. The silence was deafening. Her joke didn't seem to be funny to the royalty involved and she quickly wished she'd kept her sense of humor to herself. She glanced at Nico, biting her lip, and found that his blue eyes were sparkling with amusement at her faux pas.

"Well, there you go," he said at last, giving her a sly sideways smile. "In Rome they had circuses. In Carnethia we have the adventures of Nadia to keep us from being bored with it all. And incidentally, to keep us buying papers."

She flushed, appreciating him for making the effort to try to cover for her. The talk went on to other things, but she didn't join in again. She sat staring down at her plate and pushing her food around with her fork, but all the time, she was conscious of the prince sitting two places up from where she sat and of not much else. Her gaze met his one more time as he excused himself and left for an afternoon at the parliament.

That marvelous eyebrow rose. He made a quick gesture. Was it her imagination, or was there a special message in his eyes as he gave her one long, last look? A message that said, Marisa, I'd love to take you out into our little forest and ravish you beside the stream but I've sworn to stay away from you. You make it difficult when you sit there looking so beautiful. But I've got to be strong. Either that, or take another cold shower.

But as he made his way toward the exit, Carla leaned over to whisper to her. "I think Nico was trying to tell you you've got spinach in your teeth," she murmured confidentially.

Marisa laughed out loud. Everyone turned to look at her and her face flushed again as she gave herself a quick lecture on keeping a level head about her. She stared at the wall until he'd left the area and she could risk looking around the room again. Oh brother. She was going to have to find something to do with her time so she could hold back these crazy fantasies. If he'd had any idea what she was thinking!

She spent the evening on the computer, re-searching amnesia and coming up empty as far as solutions went. She heard the prince return in late afternoon and she stayed where she was, waiting until he'd gone to his suite before she ventured out and made her way to her own room. That was going to be her pattern from now on. She was going to avoid seeing him alone. That seemed to be her only answer to the problem.

But at least she was admitting to herself that a real problem existed. She had a crush on the prince.

She couldn't help it! She'd tried to keep from letting this happen. And she was sure it was only temporary. Once she had her memory back, she would forget all about the prince and his incredibly addictive kisses. Absolutely. No doubt about it. After all, she was armed with her little song about being the prince's plaything and she was never, ever going to let that happen to her.

Of course, it would all be a lot easier if she didn't keep thinking about those kisses and how wonderful it had felt to be in his arms. She'd been swept away both times, but she'd also noticed, both times, that he'd pulled away from her as soon as he could and his regret that he'd let himself embrace her that way was unmistakable. In other words, he was attracted to her completely against his will.

Well, she was going to make sure he didn't do anything else with her to regret. She had her own life to lead—just as soon as she found it again. And she knew she wasn't sticking around. So there was no point to getting involved with the prince. No point at all.

The next few days went by in a very similar manner. By the end of almost a week of imprisonment in the palace, she had to admit it was rather a pleasant incarceration, as that sort of thing went. Still, she was a captive, unable to do what she wanted to do when she wanted to do it or to move on with her life.

Move on to where? That was the question. There had to be a way to break this darn deadlock in her head. Where, oh where was her memory? So close and yet so far. It was very frustrating.

And yet, in some ways it was becoming irrelevant. The pattern of her days was taking on a pleasant rhythm, lulling her into a sense of normalcy she didn't deserve to feel.

And then there was the prince. There was no denying that there was a spark of something dangerous between the two of them. But so far, they'd gotten pretty good at ignoring it and letting it simmer under the surface. Still, every time her gaze met his and she felt that jolt of excitement, she got a yearning inside that was hard to ignore.

Everyone at the palace was preparing for the coronation. Nico's older brother Dane would become the new King of Carnethia. That was one reason Nico was working such long hours, and another reason security was being emphasized more and more. There were factions who would just as soon make sure that the coronation never happened.

She'd told the prince about the man she'd seen skulking behind the wall across the street from the palace. He'd sent out guards to scour the neighborhood but they hadn't found anything. Now they were going through the houses that faced the palace one by one, just in case. She felt a little guilty that she'd stirred up such a commotion, but Nico had convinced her that it had to be done. The royal family was in a defensive position, whether it wanted to be or not.

"And we still don't know what the papers sewn into my skirt are all about," she noted that afternoon after he'd told her the latest about the search. "And we still haven't found my suitcase."

He'd found her in the library, poring over the antique book section. They seemed to run into each other there more and more often lately. She was fascinated by the old cookbooks she'd found there and he was doing research into previous government actions, attempting to get a handle on what his own government was trying to accomplish today and how to avoid some of the harmful consequences of the past. They seemed to be able to meet more naturally in this room with its wonderful deep-cherry paneling and tall beveled windows, than anywhere else in the house.

"The analysts are at a dead end in identifying the symbols. They think the script is probably from an old language that hasn't been well documented yet." He turned and smiled at her as he slid a huge volume back into its place on the shelf. "Chauncy has a theory that you're an archeology student carrying documents to a museum in London. Maybe something special your professor uncovered in an ancient tomb."

She brightened. "Well, that's better than his last theory, that I was a spy." She smiled, thinking of it. How much fun it would be to be an archeology student, digging around in abandoned civilizations and making wonderful discoveries. Could she…? She gave it a moment, but nothing touched a chord or brought up a compatible memory.

So she was a bit deflated when she finally asked, "But how does that explain the amnesia?"

His eyes darkened as he looked down at her. "How do *you* explain it?"

She was tempted to say she didn't. But she really owed him some sort of attempt, so she made one.

"I think when I got knocked down on the bridge, the bump I took on my head knocked me silly." She touched where it had wounded her and was glad to feel that it had pretty much healed. "I'm assuming that it did something to jolt my memory center or something, and it just hasn't cleared up yet. But it will." At this point, she wasn't sure if she was still sounding confident or if she was beginning to show a little desperation.

"You don't think there might be a psychological component? Perhaps some reason, something you were running from, that made your mind happy to blot out reality for a time?"

She hesitated. She'd suspected something

along those lines herself, but it was a scary thing to contemplate. That was why her mind shied away from it. How did you protect yourself if you didn't know what was coming at you?

Instead of responding, she looked up at him, her helplessness in her eyes, and he moved toward her. His body language was echoing the message his eyes were conveying. He wanted to take her into his arms and hold her close and kiss her until the vulnerability evaporated and she didn't have that troubled look anymore. She lifted her face in his direction, stripped of all defense against him. She ached for him and she let it show.

He almost kissed her. He was so close, she could feel his breath on her cheek, smell his masculine scent, feel the heat of his body. His lips were inches from hers. But at the very last second, he pulled away. Looking back at her, he swore softly, turned and walked from the room.

She closed her eyes and swayed and wished she didn't care.

* * *

Though Marisa did love working in the library, the funny thing was, she seemed to have an even stronger preference for working in the kitchen and had a real affinity for cooking. Whenever she had nothing else to occupy her time, she found herself gravitating in that direction. She definitely knew how to cook, and though she hardly ever seemed to need instructions, she was having a great time incorporating recipes from the antique cookbooks she'd found in the library. She cooked up some great meals. Everyone treated her like the wonder of the year, oohing and aahing over her culinary creations, especially when it came to fancy desserts.

"You should see her in the kitchen," Carla told Nico at dinner the night she concocted a chocolate truffle marquise to die for. "She's got the whole staff whipped into shape."

"Well, they are kind of an amateur lot," Nico said, almost apologetically. "We were going to hire a French chef but we haven't gotten around to it yet."

"I think we should hire Marisa," Carla said,

waving a chocolate-stained spoon in the air. "She's better than any chef we've ever had."

By this time Nico had taken a forkful of the marquise cake and his eyes glazed over. "Wow," he said. He looked at Marisa as though he were seeing her for the first time. "Wow," he said again, and took another bite.

"See? I told you." Carla gurgled happily. "She's a chocolate genius."

"A chocolate genius." Something in that phrase seemed to zap inside Marisa's head, like a rubber band being snapped. For just a moment, she felt a bit faint.

"What is it?" The prince was up and out of his chair immediately, coming to her aid. "What is it, Marisa? What's wrong?"

She shook her head and tried to smile. "N-n-nothing. Really, I'm okay. I just felt a little light-headed for a moment. I'm fine, really."

He left her side and went back to his chair, but she could feel him watching her for the rest of the meal. His concern touched her, but at the same time, terrified her a little. How could it be that the two of them seemed to be entangled in some sort of emotional vortex when neither of them wanted to be at all?

That night she had trouble sleeping. No matter which way she tossed and turned, she couldn't get comfortable.

"This is all your fault, I'll bet," she whispered to her baby. "But you're definitely going to be worth it."

Dr. Zavier had done an ultrasound and told her it looked as if her baby was most likely a little girl. Lying there in the dark, she started going over names for her child. It was better than counting sheep.

But not good enough. She just couldn't sleep. Maybe it was because she was so hungry. Finally, in desperation, she rolled out of bed, put on a fluffy robe, and headed downstairs to the kitchen. She had only been rifling through cabinets for a few minutes when Prince Nico appeared in the doorway.

"What are you doing?" he asked.

"Oh!" She jumped. "I'm sorry. I didn't mean to disturb you." She frowned. "But what are you doing still up?"

He rubbed his neck and looked tired. "I'm still working on some things I brought home from Parliament," he said. "I didn't realize it was so late."

"You should go to bed," she said sternly, pulling her robe up tightly against her neck and glad it was thick and fluffy.

He blinked at her vehemence and for just a moment, she thought he might actually relax into a smile. "How about you?" he responded, glancing at her belly area.

"I couldn't sleep. I just need…" She bit her lip and looked at the huge stainless-steel refrigerator.

"You're hungry?" he said, incredulous. "You ate like a truck driver at dinner."

She was instantly indignant. "I did not! And besides, remember, I'm eating for two."

This time there was no doubt about it, his blue eyes had an authentic twinkle to them. "Of course." He tilted his head as though allowing her this point. "My mistake."

Nodding, she went back to going through the cupboards. "I just don't understand why there isn't any marzipan in this house," she complained.

"Marzipan?" He came closer and looked over her shoulder into the cabinet.

"Yes. How can you run a kitchen without marzipan? I've been searching all the shelves."

"Can you use a tube of almond paste instead?" he asked, reaching around her to point it out.

"Oh." She moved a little to the side. He was awfully close. "Well, it's not perfect, but I guess it will do." She took down the tube and put it on the counter. "Thanks," she said, giving him a fleeting sideways smile that quickly turned serious again. "Now, where do you suppose I could find a tin of smoked salmon?"

He choked. "Wait a minute," he said. "Marzipan and smoked salmon?"

She wrinkled her nose. "It doesn't sound right,

does it? But I don't know, it just feels like some-thing I've got to have."

"Hold everything," Nico said wisely. "You know what this is, don't you?"

She looked at him blankly. "No. What?"

He aimed a significant look at her belly. "It's the baby talking."

She grimaced. "My baby wants marzipan and salmon?"

He shrugged. "Could be. Have you ever wanted that combination before?"

Slowly, she shook her head, her gaze now caught by his in a way that sent tingles down her spine.

"I wouldn't think so," he said wryly, moving closer. "In fact, I'll bet it's pretty much a first for this kitchen."

"You think so?" she echoed, unable to pull her gaze from his.

"I do."

He was standing so close and his eyes held her mesmerized. She swallowed hard, knowing she should break the connection, but not quite able to do it.

"Let's see," he said softly, and before she knew what he was doing, he'd reached in under her robe and placed his hand on her stomach.

"Oh!" she said, but she didn't pull away. "What are you doing?"

"Shh," he said sternly. "I'm listening."

He was joking. Wasn't he? Had to be. But she stood very still, breathless, while he got a faraway look in his eyes and pretended to be channeling her baby's thoughts.

"Hmmm," he said, mouth quirking at the corners. "Smoked salmon and marzipan are just the appetizers. She wants cotton candy, bagel dogs and a pint of peppermint ice cream. Oh, and peanut butter."

Marisa's eyes grew round. "Peanut butter! Oh, yes!"

An actual grin softened his face. His hand left her belly but only to move to her chin, where he tilted her face up toward his. She looked up dreamily, held in his spell and happy to be there. Her heart was pounding and her head was light. He was going to kiss her, wasn't he? She could almost taste it and she yearned toward him as his head began to lower.

"Once this baby is born," he was murmuring, "we'll have to put in a special kitchen if these crazy food cravings continue."

It took a half second for his meaning to register. His lips had almost touched hers. But when she realized what he was saying, she drew in a sharp breath and jerked back away from him. Her hands rose to hold him off and she stared into eyes that no longer held her in their spell.

"What makes you assume I'll still be here when I give birth to my baby?" she demanded.

He drew back as well and all humor faded. His eyes were dark and unreadable. "I'm not assuming anything," he said stiffly.

"Yes, you are. You're acting as if you're sure I'm still going to be here." She moved sideways against the counter to get away from his compelling presence. "Is anything actually being done to find out who I am?"

"Marisa…"

"Nothing's happening, is it?"

"Of course things are happening. These investigations take time."

Right. She glared at him. Suddenly she was thunderstruck by the idiocy of her recent compliance with it all. She was pretending to be a guest here. How had she let herself float into this situation? She was no guest. It was high time she paid more attention to what was going on.

"Don't you have to come up with some sort of charges to keep a person against their will? Tell me, Your Highness. Am I a prisoner here?"

His mouth twisted. "Marisa, I thought we had gone over this the other day. Didn't you understand the seriousness of the problem?"

She shook her head. It was overwhelming to be surrounded by so many pitfalls and not know which way to turn. The biggest black hole that gaped in front of her was the danger of falling in love with this man. It would be so easy—and it would mean complete disaster. How to ruin your life in one simple step.

Suddenly, she felt like crying. She wanted to go home. If only she knew how.

"I don't know why I'm letting you do this," she whispered, shaking her head and holding back tears.

His frown was merciless. "You're letting me do this because you don't have any choice. Believe me, this is the best of all your options."

She knew he was right. He could have let her go to jail as a suspected spy. Instead, he'd ensconced her in this velvet prison. But that was the catch. Going through normal channels, she would have known what she had to do to get out again. Here, she wasn't so sure. How was she ever going to win her own release?

Blinded by tears, she threw him one last angry look and turned to go back to her room, forgetting all about the food her baby had ordered up. It was just as well. She wasn't hungry any more.

CHAPTER EIGHT

PRINCE Nico hit the wall and executed a perfect flip turn against the tile, then stroked strongly back across the pool, swimming as hard as he could. He'd already spent an hour in the gym, then another half hour running on the track. Now he was hoping a good hard swim would finally rid him of this aching restlessness that was driving him crazy.

He had a country to run. How the hell had he let himself get sidetracked by a pretty blonde who couldn't even remember her own name? If he were more like his brother Dane, who steamrolled through the female population like a force of nature, he would bed her and move on. If he were more like his younger brother Mychale, he would enjoy a game of sweet seduction and everyone would know it was not to be taken seriously. But he was Nico, the careful one. He'd only had one love in his life. He didn't expect ever to have another. And yet, there was something about the woman that wouldn't let him go.

It was impossible. Even if he were ready to fall in love again, she was completely wrong for the role. She was lovely and talented and a delight to be around. But who was she? Where was she from? Who were her people? And most important, perhaps—what had she done during the war?

He could hear Dane laughing at these concerns, laughing at him and his earnest ways.

"Hell, Nico. You don't have to marry the woman. Just take her to bed. That'll either whet your appetite or kill this obsession. Either way, you'll be free of this useless agony."

"Easy for you to say," he muttered, as though Dane were really there with him.

Groaning, he vaulted out of the pool and stood, dripping water in every direction. Shaking his head to get rid of some of it, feeling like a wet and shaggy dog, he opened his eyes to find himself face to face with the woman he'd been agonizing over.

"Marisa," he said, surprised.

"Oh." She was beet-red. Obviously she was seeing more of him than she'd ever expected to. She had that deer-in-the-headlights look that meant she was about to bolt for the door. "I…I was just…"

"Wait." Reaching out quickly, he grabbed her hand. "Don't go. We need to talk."

"Talk?" She sounded strangled and there was a reason for that. Standing here, staring at his beautiful wet body, she felt as though the pounding of her heart had taken over completely. She was nothing but one big, quivering hunk of womanly sensuality. Talking was not what came readily to mind in this situation. She often took this shortcut through the pool area to get to the potting shed, but she'd never encountered anyone using it before.

"Wait." Not letting go of her hand, he reached for a towel and threw it around his shoulders. "Is that better?"

"Better than what?" she murmured, still in a sensual daze. She looked up into his face. Drops of water shimmered on his eyelashes like diamonds. "Oh, Nico, I think I'd better go."

"No, I have something I need to say to you."

"Make it fast. Please?"

He pulled her hand in and pressed it against his heart. "I just want you to understand that we are doing the best we can at finding out your background. So many records were destroyed in the war. But as soon as we can clear you, we will."

That was nice. At least he seemed to take it for granted that the odds were she would be cleared. She nodded. "I know," she said softly, her gaze flickering toward where her hand rested against his gorgeous chest. She took a deep, shuddering breath. "Can I go now?"

"No." He shook his head, then steeled himself to go on. "Marisa, I guess you know I'm very strongly attracted to you. And I'm sure you understand how stupid and self-destructive that attraction is."

Her eyes widened as she looked up at him. "Well, thanks a lot."

"No, I don't mean…" He grimaced. "Oh, hell. Marisa, you know what I'm saying here. I'm only human. But I've got important things to do and I can't get caught up in an affair."

Her eyes flashed. "Well, who asked you to?"

"Marisa…"

He was in agony. His words just weren't coming out right. She could read it all in his face and she understood perfectly well. Despite everything, she smiled.

"Let me go. And stop talking. As they say, when you find yourself in a hole, the best thing to do is to stop digging."

"But Marisa…"

"Hush."

Reaching up, she threw both arms around his neck and kissed his mouth, hard. His arms came around her and he kissed her back, even harder. His body was deliciously strong and provocative and she melted against him. Staying close, he seemed to breathe in the sense of her for just a moment, then drew back, a cloud shadowing his eyes as he took in her pretty face. He touched her cheek and smiled sadly.

"Don't worry," she said, her eyes shining. "I know there's no future for us. I don't expect it."

Slipping out of his arms, she left him, savoring the tingle his kiss had left on her lips. It was a shame, really, that he was a prince, because just on a man-woman level, she had to admit, she liked what he had to offer.

The fascinating Cousin Nadia finally came to visit the palace the next night after dinner. Marisa and Carla were listening to a new CD Carla had bought during the day when Nadia breezed in with the family's younger brother Mychale in tow. They drove up in a Lamborghini and sauntered in like film stars, sending the entire household into delighted hysterics.

"We can only stay a minute," the beautiful young woman told them regretfully. Tall and thin as a runway model, she had her jet-black hair pulled back in a tight, contemporary style that accentuated her modish pose. "We're headed for the regatta at Lake Lucinder."

Mychale didn't say anything at all. He merely seemed to be escorting Nadia and standing back with an amused look of sophisticated cynicism. From what she'd heard, he seemed to spend more of his time enjoying life with the society crowd.

"Marisa, this, at last, is Nadia." Carla dragged her forward to meet the woman she'd spoken of so often.

"A pleasure to meet you, I'm sure," Nadia said with a rather bored smile and a limp handshake.

Impressed with the elegance the woman managed to display, as well as her obvious ties to royalty, Marisa was a little nervous. The royals she knew well by now seemed like regular people compared to this. Nadia knew how to project an image.

"Oh, I'm sorry," Marisa said, mortified at the thought of imposing. "I'm afraid I'm staying in your room and using your clothes."

Nadia's smile grew warmer, as though finding

a connection with the person she was meeting helped humanize the situation. "Think nothing of it. That's not my room at all—just where I park last year's frocks." She waved a casual hand, her gaze skimming over the loose summer dress Marisa wore with a sign of recognition. "Take them all. I'll never use them again."

"Oh." Marisa was fumbling for words when Nico came into the room.

"Hello, Nadia."

Everything stood still as he regarded his cousin with a jaundiced eye. For the first time, Nadia herself showed a hint of anxiety.

"Oh, Nico. I thought you'd be off at a business meeting tonight. You usually work later than this." Her smile looked a bit strained. "Shouldn't you be out revitalizing the economy of our country or something?"

"I do my best," he said, still gazing at her with a cool, level regard.

"So I hear."

"And I hear you are doing your best to revitalize the discotheque scene in Paris."

Nadia smiled nervously. "You heard about that, did you?"

"Your escapade at the Club Giroux? Doing a striptease on a table top? Yes, I heard about it."

"It was a mock striptease," she protested. "I didn't take off my bra and panties."

Nico's gaze darkened coldly. "You're to be commended for your high moral standards."

Nadia licked her lips and tried to smile in her usual carefree fashion, but it was obvious she was not enjoying this. "I suppose Dane called and told you about it."

"Actually, no. I saw it in the paper." The beautiful woman winced. "Nadia, do you understand how important it is to stay out of the papers? We're trying to rebuild a good country here and we need the firm support and respect of the people to do it. That can all be ruined if we become an object of scorn and ridicule and lose the support of the powers that be in the media."

Nadia pretended to be interested in looking over her latest nail job. "I've already heard this entire lecture from Dane."

"So he did talk to you?"

"Oh yes." She looked up at him, trying to maintain a bit of defiance in her attitude. "By the end of our conversation he was on the phone to the Bastille, trying to find out if they had an old leftover torture rack he could borrow." She rolled her eyes. "We did not part on friendly terms."

Nico stared at her for a moment, then seemed to relax a bit. "I take it the rack wasn't available."

"No, and I guess that's what made him so irritable."

Nico bit back a smile that threatened to soften his face. "Well, he's right, Nadia. We have to stay out of the tabloids."

"I understand." She looked at him and smiled tremulously, all defiance gone. "And from now on I'll work very hard at it. I'll be as anonymous as a church mouse at the regatta."

Everybody grinned at the thought of Nadia fading into the background. Wasn't going to happen.

"You'll be with her?" Nico asked his younger brother, Mychale.

Mychale's smile was laced with cynical amusement. "I'll keep her in line," he promised.

"I hope you do." His lip curled just a bit. "Sometimes I wonder if you're not as bad as she is. Some of the things I've heard about your exploits…"

"Gross exaggerations, every one," Mychale responded lazily, but Marisa detected a flash of anger in his eyes all the same. Evidence suggested the brothers had issues. "The papers love a good story, especially if they've made it up themselves."

Nico nodded, looking as though he had more to say but had decided to hold his tongue. He excused himself to get back to working on something in the library and the two visitors didn't stay much longer. Truth to tell, everything seemed a little deflated once they'd gone.

"They just seem larger than life, those two," Lady Julia murmured.

Marisa agreed with her, but her mind was on Nico. He'd looked tired during dinner and she had a feeling the visit from Nadia and Mychale had disturbed him somehow. Still, he seemed fine when he came out to get some papers from his suite and stopped by where she was helping Carla fold some antique linens for packing in storage boxes.

Carla had been explaining some of the reasons behind her family's dread of the tabloids.

"You know very well they are constantly in search of scandal among the royals. They love to stir things up. Look what they've done in other countries."

"Can't you just ignore them?" Marisa asked.

"I wish. But you really can't. People believe the ugly things they put out. It can destabilize an entire regime."

"Really?" Marisa was skeptical.

"Oh yes. Just look at what they are doing to my brother Dane right now. They've got this bee in their bonnet about the succession. He hasn't even been crowned yet and they are already worried about whether he can have children or not."

"What?"

"Yes. You see, there is a rumor that he's had war wounds which…well, make it impossible for him to have children. So they are obsessed with trying to figure out if he's already had a child with someone. It's all so crazy."

It was at this juncture that Nico stopped by and all talk of the tabloid trash evaporated quickly. He touched the linens they were folding, asked a couple of questions about the methods of storage, then turned to Marisa.

"What did you think of Nadia?" he asked her. "Was she all you'd hoped?"

Marisa laughed. "Every bit. And very generous, too, to offer me the use of the clothes in the wardrobe."

His hard face softened. "She's a sweetheart, really," he said. "She just thinks she has to create excitement wherever she goes. We're hoping she grows up soon, before something spectacular happens." He frowned. "And now with Mychale egging her on, that might be delayed a while."

"Oh, Nico, they'll be fine," Carla said, taking

a stack of linens that had been deemed suitable for current use and carrying them off to the linen closet.

Nico watched her go, then turned back to Marisa.

"One thing I appreciate about you is that you're a good counterweight to Nadia. It's good for Carla to see that there is another style that's more down-to-earth and still attractive."

She flushed. "What a wonderful thing to say. But I'm not royal."

"You have a natural nobility that's a lot more important."

She was speechless. He went on, talking about plans for Carla during the coronation, but Marisa was hardly listening. She couldn't get over what he'd just said. Did that mean he'd decided she probably wasn't a spy after all?

He was back on the subject of Nadia, talking about how she'd come to live with the family most of the time, since her parents had died, and that brought up the topic of Mychale.

"Your little brother is quite something," Marisa noted, stashing the last of the linens in a box.

"What a cosmopolitan-looking young man. And so handsome."

Nico flashed her a look. "More handsome than I am?"

"Why, you're vain!" Marisa smiled with delight. "Who knew?"

"I am not. I was just joking." He smiled, then cocked his famous eyebrow. "But you still haven't answered my question."

That eyebrow still gave her chills. "Whether you or your brother is more handsome?" Studying him, she pretended to think it over. "You're more muscular, I think," she teased. "Harder. Stronger."

He flexed his biceps and she found herself laughing as she reached out to touch the closest bulge. The feeling of hard muscle beneath his cotton shirt was provocative in a way she hadn't expected. Suddenly her breath was a little harder to draw in. She looked up into his eyes, then quickly pulled her hand away. Swallowing, she tried to go on with the mock critique.

"But Mychale has that young, slender charm,

like a greyhound," she said quickly, her tone a little forced. "And a profile a Roman would envy."

"Now you don't like my profile?" he asked her, his eyes knowing and as cynical as his younger brother's.

"Oh no," she said breathlessly. "I like your profile very much."

He took her hand in his and brought it to his lips. "And I like yours," he said huskily, holding her with his gaze. "And I like your mouth," he added softly, moving closer. "And your kinky hair. And the pulse that beats at the base of your throat. And…"

They both heard Carla coming back and drew apart. He dropped her hand, gave her a wistful smile and turned to go. "I like it all," he said as he left, mystifying Carla. "Don't change a thing."

There was a buzzing in her ears. Carla chatted as usual, but Marisa couldn't manage more than an occasional smile. It was a good half an hour before she had her pulse back down to normal. This was nuts. She was letting him get to her and she'd sworn she wouldn't do that.

She made herself busy for the next hour, but all the time she knew he was in the library, and finally she found herself heading there.

"I'm just going to look in and see if he needs anything," she told herself, knowing she was lying but unable to help it.

She hesitated in the doorway, then took a deep breath and stepped in. He was there, working over a pile of books. Aloof and morose, he seemed like a different person from the one who had teased her. He barely looked up, and when he did, he hardly seemed to see her. In the end, she just smiled and retreated again. But her sympathy was with him. He worked so hard and had so much on his shoulders—the welfare of an entire country. She began to wrack her brain, trying to think of something that might cheer him up. Finally she had to admit, she could only think of one thing.

Chocolate.

"You're being an idiot," she told herself helplessly as she marched to the kitchen. "He doesn't want chocolate!"

"You don't know that," her chocolate-fanatic side retorted. "Besides, do you have a better idea?"

She didn't. But she did have a good ganache going on the stove—and some freshly picked strawberries from the garden. Working quickly, she cut off the tops, then cored the berries and stuffed them with the truffle ganache. After melting discs of white dipping chocolate, she drenched the berries, then with melted bitter-sweet dark chocolate, she painted little jackets with bow ties and buttons over the white "shirts." She stuck the green tops back on with white chocolate for "hair" and ended up with what looked like fat little men wearing tuxedos.

Looking at the final results, she smiled. They were cute as heck. Before she had time to think better of it, she slid two of them onto a small silver dish and headed for the library.

She looked in. Nico was leaning over the pile of opened books, his eyes tired and bloodshot, his shirt open at the neck, his hair rumpled as though he'd spent a lot of time thrusting his fingers through it. He was frowning down at his papers. Her heart began to pound. Was he going to order her out? Or ask her what on earth made her think he would want this kind of interruption? Or, even worse, give her a faint smile and pretend to appreciate what she'd made him, then politely dismiss her? For a fleeting moment, she wished she hadn't done this. But it was too late to back out now.

"Here," she said, putting the silver dish down in front of him. "I brought you something."

He looked up, his eyes moody and unreceptive. Looking at what she'd put in the dish, he straightened. A reluctant smile just barely broke the line of his mouth.

"That's very nice," he said. "Very clever." He looked at her. "Why didn't you bring them out for dessert so everybody could see them?"

"I didn't make them for everybody," she said, looking down into his eyes. "Just for you."

Leaning back in his chair, he looked at her warily, as though he was afraid to let her see what he felt. "Marisa," he said softly. "Oh, Marisa." His hand caught hers and he pulled her down into his lap. He looked at her face for a long time before he softly kissed her lips. "You're a special woman, Marisa," he said. "I wish…"

His eyes clouded and he didn't finish that thought. Putting a hand to the side of his face, she leaned close and kissed him.

"You're a pretty special man," she said, her voice husky with unshed tears. Rising from his lap, she looked back at him longingly, and left the room.

His unstated wish stayed with her into the night. She probably wished pretty much the same thing he did. But neither one of them could say it out loud.

The next morning at breakfast, the talk was all about the surprise visitors the night before. The young cousins from Belgrade hadn't been there to see them and had to be told all about it.

"Maybe *we* could go to the regatta," one said hopefully.

They both looked toward Nico as the rule-keeper and plan-maker.

"Sorry," he said, dashing their hopes. "You'd have to stay overnight and you've both got classes tomorrow."

They pouted, but there was no question that Nico's word was final. Looking across the table, Marisa felt a little sorry for them. But their request gave her an idea and she followed Nico out into the garden a few minutes later as he prepared to go for his morning run.

"I've been thinking," she said, trying not to notice once again how good he looked in shorts and a tank top. "We don't seem to be getting anywhere on my memory problem. The analysts aren't coming up with anything on the papers from my skirt. We're at a standstill and I'm really getting antsy about this. I think I should go out and mix with the populace a bit. Wander the streets. See if I recognize anything or if anyone recognizes me."

He gazed at her skeptically. "The better to run away from us?" he suggested softly as he began stretching for his run.

A flash of anger raced through her. After all

this time, did he still think she was a liar and a cheat?

"No, Nico," she said firmly. "And if you think so poorly of me, I guess there's not much use in…"

"Hold on," he said, reaching out and taking her by the shoulders and gazing deeply into her eyes. "I don't think poorly of you at all. Not a bit. Surely you know that."

His hands slid down her arms, fingers caressing her flesh, and then he jerked away as though he'd pulled himself from the brink of doing something he knew he shouldn't. Turning away from her, he reached for his towel.

"But I wouldn't blame you if you were getting impatient to get out of the palace and try something new," he said quickly. "And that's why I thought you might like to go with us to the Carnethian National Derby Cup this weekend."

She blinked. "You mean the run of the horses at Brolney that we hear about in legend and song?"

"Yes."

Her heart jumped. That sounded like fun. "I don't think I've ever been."

His half grin was infectious. "It would be surprising if you had. It hasn't been held for the last fifty years."

"Oh." She laughed.

"Dane is still in Paris so I'll have to go to represent the family. It's important to bring back these old traditions in order to help the people feel that they really have their country back." He gave her a look. "I think you would enjoy it."

"You think so?" It was funny how such a simple thing could raise such expectations. She was feeling like a new person.

"Carla's coming. So why don't you come along too? You could use a diversion."

She wanted to hug him, she was so happy. "I-I'd love to."

He was still looking at her with that half-bemused, half-affectionate expression, as though he'd decided he couldn't pretend he didn't like her after all. "I know it's been rough on you all this week," he added.

She wanted to laugh and dance and kiss him. "No, actually, it's been very pleasant. Carla is a darling and the food is good and…" She couldn't really add that the host was sexy and romantic and made her blood sing, could she?

"We'll have to keep your pregnancy covered up as much as possible at the races," he was saying with a thoughtful frown. "We don't want to start any rumors."

That stopped her in her tracks. "What sort of rumors?"

He looked at her sideways and put the towel around his neck. "A pregnant woman is always the hub of rumor central, especially when she's staying at the palace. Surely you can see that."

She frowned, her lovely mood dimming. "I suppose so."

"You'll be there as Carla's friend," he said, making it up as he went along. "Who could take exception to Carla bringing a friend along?"

He stopped and looked at her, glancing down at her rounded belly.

"How are you feeling?" he asked, obviously referring to her pregnancy.

"Very well. No complaints." She smiled, hand

192 THE PRINCE'S SECRET BRIDE

on her tummy. Dr. Zavier had stopped in the day before and given her a checkup. He seemed to think everything was proceeding normally. "Lots of moving. No real firm kicks yet, but once that happens, I'll make you try to feel it. Okay?"

She held her breath. The question was more important than she'd realized as she was asking it, and now the answer was the most important thing in the world. Did he want to feel her baby kick? Or did he want to distance himself from the whole thing?

He was impassive for a long moment, and then he smiled.

"Okay."

His smile was so natural and genuine, it made her heart skip a beat. And then he was off, jogging past the garden as he headed for the perimeter of the property. She watched him go, enjoying the beauty of his muscles at work and the way his dark hair caught the sunlight, savoring him as though she knew she was going to have nothing left of him but memories very soon.

* * *

Carla was excited about the plans for the weekend. So were the Belgrade cousins, Jan and Jols.

"This is even better than the regatta!" one of them crowed.

"The only thing more exciting will be the St. Tupin's Day Ball next month," said the other.

"There's a ball next month?" Marisa asked Carla as they walked out to the day parlor.

"Oh yes. It's basically for me. I've got to come out. And Dane thinks we should do it before the coronation."

"You're not out? I thought you high-society girls did that at about eighteen."

"We do," Carla said, batting Marisa with a tea towel for using the term. "All things being equal, I would have come out a long time ago, except the war got in the way the last few years. So now, we're having a great big ball. It's so exciting! Lady Julia is going to present me." She sighed. "I feel a little foolish, of course, being so old and all. But you notice I'm not married, or even engaged, so it's assumed I'd better put myself out there."

"Carla! They'll be standing in line."

"Hmm. Maybe. We'll see, I suppose." She looked at Marisa speculatively. "But I have a favor to ask you. If everything turns out okay and you're not a spy and all, would you be my official companion at the ball?"

Marisa blanched. "Oh Carla, I'm bound to be aggressively showing by then."

"I don't care." Carla smiled at her with candid affection. "Spy or not, preggers or not, you're the best friend I've ever had. And I want you there." Her big eyes turned to puppy-dog pleading. "Please say yes."

Marisa took her hands and held them. She was very fond of the girl and wanted to do anything she could to make her happy. It broke her heart to think that she had no friends to speak of. She only wondered if Carla realized how tentative her stay here really was. She wasn't supposed to be a friend. She was actually a prisoner. Why was everyone skipping that part?

"Of course I'll be there if it is at all possible. I promise."

And she bit her lip, wondering if she'd just become a liar.

They spent the afternoon planning for the trip and deciding on their wardrobes. Marisa had a great selection as Nadia spent a lot of time going to special events and had the clothes to wear to them. She finally picked out a day outfit of a navy blue shift with a white jacket, and red-and-blue scarf at the neck—very chic in a preppy way. Carla was going through one outfit after another and still couldn't decide.

"I'm supposed to be thinking about being attractive to a possible marriage prospect," she fretted. "Dane thinks I should dress like a nun. Mychale says be trendy. Aunt Julia counsels a little cleavage." She rolled her eyes.

Marisa laughed. "What does Nico say?"

"He's the only one who says, 'Be yourself.'" She looked doleful. "But he doesn't really mean it. I'm supposed to zero in on someone upright and smart and educated—but royal—and make him fall in love with me. That's not so easy, you know."

"No, I wouldn't think so." She felt a pang of

sympathy for the girl. "Does he really have to be royal?"

"Yes. Dane is very keen on us all marrying royalty, just to help shore up our credibility as a country."

Marisa had another pang of sympathy, and this time for herself. But that was silly. She didn't have a chance in the world of marrying royalty herself. So what did she care?

"How many eligible royals are there?" she asked.

"Oh, tons. There are all kinds of royals all over."

Marisa raised a skeptical eyebrow, sure she must be overstating the case a bit.

"The trick is to find one who isn't a pampered playboy," Carla said with a sigh, "someone serious and decent, like my brothers."

Marisa nodded at that, helping Carla put her things back on hangers. From what she'd seen, Nico was one hard-working man. Mychale seemed to be another story, but from all accounts Dane was a lot like Nico. Growing up in exile and then fighting to get your country back probably had something to do with producing that sort of man.

"Of course, it would help if I was pretty," Carla said so softly, at first Marisa wasn't sure she'd heard her right.

"What? What are you talking about? You're beautiful!"

"Oh Marisa, don't try to fool me. I've got mirrors."

"You've got mirrors, but no experience," Marisa said firmly. "Just because your style of looks may not be the most popular at the moment, doesn't mean it won't be soon. Style is always in state of flux. The trick is to learn how to use whatever you've got to your own advantage."

"Hmm." Carla looked skeptical. "Be specific."

Marisa was at a loss for a moment, then nodded slowly. "Tell you what. We'll give it our all for the derby. Okay? We'll get your hairstylist in here, and a makeup artist, and see what we can do."

"Really?" Carla looked as though she was hesitant to let herself get too excited. "You promise?"

"I promise." Marisa gave the younger girl a hug. "Time to turn into a butterfly, Carla. You just wait and see."

Nico was quiet at dinner. Carla and the Belgrade cousins did most of the talking, chattering about other derbys they had attended in the past. Marisa tried to join in the general hilarity, but her gaze kept straying to where Nico sat, looking like a man with a lot on his mind. It seemed trivial to talk about pleasure outings when he seemed to be thinking about how to save Carnethian society.

Or was it something more than that? Something more personal? Something more tragic?

Later in the evening, after a game of cards with the others, she was wandering through the house and noticed he'd gone out in the twilight and was sitting at the edge of the grass, staring into the forest, nursing a drink.

"Just leave it alone, Marisa," she told herself fiercely. "He doesn't need you prying into his business. And if he wanted comfort, he wouldn't hesitate to ask for it, would he?"

But she ached inside to see him looking so tormented.

Finally she couldn't stand it any longer. She had to go out.

He looked up as she came near, watching her approach without smiling or making any sign of welcome.

"Nico, what's wrong?" she asked, standing over him.

"Wrong?" He waved his drink in the air. "Why do you ask? Nothing's wrong."

She stared down at him for a moment, then dropped to sit beside him in the grass. "In the evening sometimes you get such a haunted look in your eyes," she said hesitantly, ready to drop this line of conversation if he gave the slightest indication that he hated it. "It looks as though…well, as though you have bad memories."

His head went back and he scowled at her. "Bad memories? Are you kidding? We just went through five years of fighting to restore our monarchy, Marisa. Lots of ugly things happened. Sure I've got bad memories."

She winced. "You have to put them behind you." She hesitated. What was she doing? All things being equal, she ought to know better. Here she was, a nobody with no credentials whatsoever trying to give advice to her country's prince, second in line to the throne. But when she saw him like this, he was just a man. A man she felt a deep connection to, for no logical reason.

"You can't let those bad memories distort the life you have to live now," she added, wishing she could think of some less trite way of putting it.

He stared off at the forest again. "Some things can't be cast off so easily. We can't all have your luck with amnesia."

His tone wasn't friendly, but it wasn't hostile. She took a deep breath and decided to go for broke.

"Is it Andrea?"

He turned quickly, staring at her. "Who told you about Andrea?"

"No one. You called me that name the first night I was here."

A storm was brewing in his blue eyes, but he

didn't say another word. After staring at her for a long moment, he set his glass down in the grass and rose, walking off into the dark forest, leaving her behind.

She stayed where she was, wishing life wasn't so confusing, wishing bad things didn't happen to good people. But they did. All the time.

It was almost a quarter of an hour before he came back. He stopped on the walkway, looking at her, and she was sure he was going to go on in without speaking. But after a moment or two, he turned and walked slowly her way and dropped down onto the grass beside her again.

"Andrea grew up in France," he began without preamble, "like a lot of our exile community. Her father was a big backer of the royal family. Think of your stereotyped picture of a French World-War-Two resistance fighter and you've got a sense of what Andrea looked like."

Despite himself, his voice, which had started out harsh and cold, began to soften with a sense of lost affection.

"She was fearless. Over that last year when

the fighting was getting very intense, we lived together in the mountains and fought side by side. We tempted fate and took such chances." He shook his head as though he could hardly believe it now. "We fell in love." His voice broke. "We made a child. I wanted her to go back to Paris where she would be safe, but she wouldn't hear of it. She had to be on the front lines of the rebellion." He half smiled, his eyes on the past, remembering. "In fact, I was furious with her there toward the end. She was carrying our child." His voice rose. "She should have been more careful. It was not just her own life she was risking.…"

His voice grew very rough and he stopped for a moment, his eyes closed, composing himself.

"She was hit by a sniper's bullet and then she was dead," he said in a more business-like fashion. "They were both dead. I didn't really have time to grieve at first. We were under attack day and night. I was pretty sure I would be dead, too, before it was all over. It wasn't until we routed the enemy and took over the city that I really had time to sit back and take account of what had been lost. And then I grieved." His voice thickened again. "She was so young, so beautiful, so full of grit and goodness. Our country lost so much when she died. The world lost. For a while, I thought I would go out of my mind with grief."

He paused, closing his eyes and letting the emotion pass. Marisa couldn't know exactly how he felt, but she had a pretty good idea, and she ached for him. Tears welled in her eyes and she bit her lip to keep from letting out a sound.

"But I didn't," he said at last. "I'm still here, still sane. But the pain is always there as well."

"Especially in the evening," she ventured quietly.

"Yes, for some reason." He shrugged. "Especially in the evening."

They were both quiet for a moment, digesting all he'd said. Finally, Marisa said softly, "I'm so sorry."

He turned to her. Reaching up, he soaked up the tears running down her cheeks with his finger.

"I know," he said softly. "I'm sorry too. Everyone's sorry." His hand cupped her chin and he looked down into her warm dark eyes.

"Do you think that you'll ever be able to love that way again?" she asked shakily.

It was a crazy question to ask. Insane. Pathetic. There was no hope for her, no matter how much she might dream. She closed her eyes, wishing she'd kept her emotions to herself. She was only going to drive him away with questions like that.

But he didn't pull away. Though he frowned, he began to trace her lips with his finger.

"I didn't think so. I was sure, in fact. Until…"

She opened her eyes. What was he saying? She could hardly breathe. "Until?" she asked, unable to let it lie there.

Instead of answering, he kissed her gently, tasting her lips as though testing them. Then he leaned back and looked into her face.

"You'd better go in, Marisa," he told her softly. "The night is full of magic and I'm feeling a little crazy."

Looking into his eyes, all she could think of

were violins and satin sheets—and a man's hard hand trailing hot excitement down the length of her body. She didn't want to go in. She wanted to hold him with her heart and comfort him with her body. Was it finally time for her to admit it? She was in love with this man.

How had she let this happen? She'd tried to guard against it from the first. She knew there was no future in it. He was royal, for God's sake. And she was not about to let herself be a prince's plaything.

"Tomorrow we are taking you out into the world," he noted, his eyes darkly shadowed in the muted light. "Who knows what will happen? Maybe we'll see someone who remembers you."

She turned to look at him. She knew she could make one simple move and be in his arms. She could feel his desire, could barely conceal her own. He was being a gentleman, but his sensual response lay just beneath the surface and she could coax it out easily. One word, one move, and she could have him. The protection of the forest wasn't far away.

Why not? She wanted to. She ached to feel his strength, to take him in her body and give him all she had to give. If she did it, she would always have a tiny piece of him, a memory.

But that would be all she would ever get. And she knew now how slippery memories could be.

Closing her eyes, she gathered herself together and decided to do what was right. With a sigh, she turned and smiled at him. "Good night," she whispered.

He touched her cheek with his hand, then drew it back and stared past her at the trees. He had a quick fantasy of chucking it all and grabbing Marisa and heading for Tahiti—never looking back. Could people still hide out in the South Seas? They could live on the beach and go spearfishing for food. She would look cute in a little grass skirt.

But he knew he wasn't going to do that. He'd spent his life preparing for the restoration of his family to power. Now their dreams had come true and he was going to throw it all away because he had fallen helplessly in love.

Fallen in love. Was that really what he'd done? And if so, who cared? He couldn't do anything about it. He was committed to this job, this country, his family. He couldn't possibly betray them all for a woman. Even a woman like this.

"Tonight may be the last night we have you here," he said softly, his fingers combing through her hair, his hand cupping her head.

"No," she said, a note of near panic in her voice. "Oh no."

"It's possible," he said. "So, just in case…"

He leaned closer and kissed her again. She forgot all about her plans to do the right thing. His kiss was hot and hard and she was dizzy. No room for thought. All she needed to do was feel. She closed her eyes and sank into the kiss, the embrace, the emotion that was building between them. She wanted nothing but him.

"Marisa? Are you out there?" Carla's voice cut through their private moment like a knife.

Nico groaned, pulling back, and Marisa took a deep breath and hoped her voice wouldn't choke in her throat. "Over here, Carla," she called.

"Oh good. Come in quick. The stylists are here. We've got to go over plans for tomorrow."

Nico dropped a quick kiss on her trembling lips and smiled in the darkness. "Good night, Marisa," he said softly. "Dream of me."

CHAPTER NINE

AFTER breakfast the next morning, Marisa wandered into the library, drawn, as usual, to the cookbooks. It would be another hour or so before they left for the races and she had some time to kill. She pulled down a particularly decrepit specimen on yellowed parchment, one of the ones she hadn't looked through before. It was probably the oldest one she'd seen yet. Hundreds of years old. She handled it carefully, afraid to tear the sheets. Studying page after page, she could barely make out the words. In some sections, the symbols didn't even seem to be letters. Could this be a real language? She didn't recognize it as such. In fact, the symbols reminded her of…

Her jaw dropped. She stared at the page for a

long, long moment, digesting what this might just mean. Then she grabbed the book to her chest and began to run through the house, searching for Nico.

There didn't seem to be anybody about. She found Chauncy in the butler's pantry, but he was busy on the phone making the weekly grocery order and waved her off. The maids didn't have a clue, but it seemed everyone else was dressing for their outing.

Finally, trepidatious but too full of her news to wait, she ran up the stairs to the prince's suite and knocked on the door. There was no answer. Cautiously, she tried the doorknob. It opened easily to her touch. She stepped inside.

"Nico?" she called, closing the door behind her. "Marisa?"

His voice came from the bathroom.

"Just a minute."

And then he was walking into the room, clad only in a small white towel he was holding at his waist, water from his shower still glistening on his shoulders.

She gasped and tried to turn away, but just couldn't do it.

He smiled. "This isn't real, is it?" he teased. "You haven't really shown up in my bedroom. I'm dreaming, aren't I?"

She shouldn't have come here. This could take her right down the road she'd vowed not to go on. She started to back away. "Oh, Nico, I'm sorry, I didn't realize…"

"See? My dreams never work out like they should," he said lightly. "And here I thought you'd come to tell me you couldn't live without my gloriously sculpted body any longer."

She was bright red, half-laughing, half-appalled. He was joking but his words were cutting too near the bone for comfort. The cookbook hung forgotten from her fingers. She'd never seen anything more beautiful than this man's body.

"I'd better go," she stuttered out. "I'll come back when you're…"

"Dressed? Turn around. It'll only take a minute."

She turned around, and she closed her eyes for good measure. Not because she was shy. More because she could hardly breathe and was afraid if she saw too much more of him, she might go into an embarrassing swoon. Not to mention lose all ability to resist throwing herself at his feet.

"Okay," he said.

She turned back, then closed her eyes again, scrunching them tightly. "You're going to have to put a shirt on, too," she warned him. "I've got my standards, you know."

He laughed. "Okay, Miss Manners, I'm fully clothed. Your honor is safe, and so is mine."

Opening her eyes, she sighed, thinking of lost opportunities. He still looked good in slacks and a shirt, but something was lost as far as the more carnal senses were concerned.

"Look," she said, remembering what she'd come for. "I was looking through the cookbooks in your library and look what I found."

She spread the book open to the page with the symbols. Nico bent over it and recognized what it was right away.

"It looks like the same style of writing," he said. "Good lord, how old is this thing?"

"Hard to tell. But it looks like something from medieval times, doesn't it?"

"Something very old, dug out of a historical trash heap. Very interesting."

Turning to a tall closet, he opened the door and pulled out a flat drawer, then carefully removed the papers which had been sewn into her skirt.

"Here we go," he said. "Let's compare and contrast, shall we?"

He laid the papers next to the book. They both stared down at the symbols, going from one to the other. Marisa felt prickles on the back of her neck. This was spooky. Raising her head, she met his gaze and they stared at each other.

"They're the same, aren't they?" she said in wonder.

He nodded. "This is the breakthrough we've been waiting for," he said. Reaching over, he picked up his phone. "Get me Trendyce at Intelligence," he said into the receiver. "I've got some new information here."

"Do you think this will help interpret those papers from my skirt?" she asked him.

"No doubt about it." He smiled at her. "You did good, Marisa. This is a great find. I'll give this to Trendyce and he'll get his analysts on it right away."

She nodded, feeling pleased. "I hope it does the trick," she said, glancing back regretfully as she turned to go. "And now, in more than one way, I guess we're off to the races."

Marisa was pretty sure she'd never arrived at an event in a convoy of long black limousines escorted by heavily uniformed men on motorcycles before. That was quite an experience in itself. Colorful banners in blue, yellow and red were flying everywhere. The scene looked as though it was set for a medieval jousting match. People lined the streets and waved little flags, calling out as they passed. She almost felt famous. And that was pretty funny, when she was actually anonymous, even to herself.

The racetrack was in the process of being restored from war damage. There was a new central receiving area with turrets and gold-leaf embellishments on the pillars. They were led in through the main gates, then onto the stand and up the red-carpeted stairs for access to the royal box.

The royal box might have been a conference room in a five-star hotel, with thick carpets and large, plush seating for about twenty people. It also had the best vantage of the field. Waiters stood ready with trays holding glasses of champagne and plates with crudités. The royal party was seated, and they all looked around expectantly. It was all so luxurious, they felt truly pampered.

Visitors came and went, though each went through security first. Carla began to meet some of the young men who had come to pay their respects to the very eligible princess. Marisa looked on happily, feeling just a little smug. Carla looked gorgeous. Instead of wearing her hair in a clump pushed back behind her ears and hanging down her back like a thicket, the way she usually did, Marisa had encouraged the stylist to give her a dramatic cut, even though the princess had squealed in horror at the thought. Now her hair was just below chin length and cut to frame the girl's face in a way that set off her pale eyes and her pretty mouth. A makeup artist had done a little magic to her face. Marisa had helped her choose her outfit for the day, a silky pant suit that hid her tendency toward plumpness. She looked lovely and she was busy developing the kind of confidence that would hold her in good stead in the hunt for a mate suitable for royalty.

That thought gave Marisa a twinge, but she pushed it aside and went on. An employee in tails came into the box with a racing form and everyone placed small bets on their favorites.

"I don't know who any of them are," she told Nico with a frown.

"It's more fun if you place a bet or two," he advised her.

"But how do I choose?"

"You could close your eyes and point," he said. "Or you could look at the names and try to find one you can relate to. Pull something out of your life."

"That's not so easy when your own past is a mystery to you," she reminded him.

"Nothing rang a bell on the drive over?" he asked, looking at her closely and wishing he could nibble on her ear.

"No. Not a thing." They had driven through the city, then along the lake and into the mountains, and nothing had meant a thing to her.

"Then look at the names and just pick something."

She glanced down the list. "Oh, I don't know. Hmm. There's a horse named Piccolo. I had a cat named Piccolo when I was a little girl."

She looked up, realizing what she'd just said. Nico was staring back at her.

"What did you say?" he asked incredulously.

She gasped. "I remembered something from my past," she said, getting excited. "Oh Nico! I remembered something."

He gave her a long, slow smile, enjoying her candid joy. "Great. Now take it easy. Don't try to force anything. Just let it come naturally."

"Okay," she promised, but she was more

excited than Christmas morning. Piccolo. She could see that little black cat now. She looked back down at the race list but her mind refused to see it. She was trying hard not to try to remember but she just couldn't help it. The trouble was, nothing else was coming to her. She closed her eyes. Still nothing.

Oh well. She dismissed the whole attempt. She was bound and determined she was going to have a good time today. No disappointing thoughts. She would just try the remembering later on, when the races were over.

The first race was run. Piccolo came in last. Marisa frowned, wondering if that was an omen. But everyone was having a good time, chatting and laughing, and she sat where she could watch Nico and she had to admit she enjoyed that. He was so handsome and gracious to those who came by to talk to him. He seemed to be having fun, too. The worried look was erased for the day, and that was good to see.

Another race was run, and then they were served custard with berry sauce topping, a national dish. Marisa sat beside Carla and watched her begin to try a little flirting with her visitors. Laughing, she egged her on. One handsome swain, introduced as Jans Hunsinger from Amsterdam, a friend of Nadia's, was particularly attentive.

"Princess Carla, your beauty far exceeds all the reports we've had. Why have they been keeping you under wraps?"

Carla blushed under such brutally blunt admiration and looked to Marisa for help.

"The princess has been fully involved in the liberation of Carnethia," Marisa explained. "She hasn't had time for social frivolity. Now that the war is over, she's hoping to have a little fun."

Jans smiled in a practiced sexy way that showed off more guile than sincerity. "Your Highness, I have to admit, fun is practically my middle name. I'd love to show you the highlights in a nighttime tour of the city. Allow me to leave my card with your party. You can call me on a moment's notice. I can personally guarantee that you will have a good time."

"That would be wonderful," Carla said, obviously smitten.

Jans's gaze flickered over Marisa. "And who is this lovely lady accompanying you?"

"Oh, this is my friend Marisa. She's staying with us right now."

He gave her a silky smile and took her hand in his. His gaze traveled down and quickly returned to meet hers, but she knew he had noticed her pregnancy. A scowl from Nico was warning him his visiting time was up. "Lucky girl," he said. "I hope to be allowed to visit you myself one day."

"Oh, I'm sure you will," Carla said. "Maybe Nadia can bring you by."

Nico and Marisa exchanged a look as Jans took his leave. It was evident neither one of them thought much of the young man, but Carla was in ecstasy.

"Wasn't he gorgeous? Oh, Marisa! How can I make sure he's invited to the ball?"

"I guess you can check with the social secretary to see if he's on the list," Marisa said doubtfully.

Another race was about to be run and Aunt
Julia had neglected to place a bet.

"I'll do it for you," Marisa offered. She had a
yen to walk around a little anyway.

Taking Aunt Julia's pick, she set off to find the
betting window. It was exciting being in the
crowd, listening to the talk and feeling a part of
it all. The line was short and she quickly reached
the window and placed the bet. As she was
turning back toward the box, she was caught up
in a group heading for the railing to watch the race
and pushed along like a leaf in the current of the
ocean. Suddenly a rough hand grabbed her arm
and pulled her to the side and there was a voice
in her ear as a man leaned close from behind.

"Well, Marie, you've certainly landed yourself
on a fine perch, haven't you?"

She tried to turn to see who was speaking, but
the crowd surged and she was forced to move
forward with the man still gripping her arm.

"Let me go," she said loudly, trying to pull away.

The man didn't release her arm. She looked
around for help, but no one was paying any at-

tention. Icy fear crept through her. How was she going to get away from this man?

"Listen, Marie," he said, leaning close. "Umberto says all will be forgiven if you just give him a call. Better do it very soon. Bad things will happen if you don't."

She tried again to twist around to see him, and what she saw didn't reassure her. His features were even and not unpleasant, but he had the hardest, coldest eyes she'd ever seen. She didn't have a clue who he might be.

"Take care, my girl," he said. "One day you'll fly alone and we have a nice cage we're saving just for you."

He dropped his grip on her and left as suddenly as he'd appeared, melting into the crowd. She rubbed her arm where he'd been holding her and pushed her way through the mob to get back to the royal box. For just a moment she wondered if she really wanted to tell Nico what had happened. The man knew her. He was rough and uncouth. What if she was part of a bunch of con artists or something more awful? What would happen if Nico found out she was a crook or some sort of criminal? How long would he still be interested in knowing her?

But she really didn't have any choice in the matter. Looking at him as she entered the box, she felt a flood of emotion—relief, fear, anxiety. He was the one she had to go to.

"What's wrong?" He could see the agitation in her face right away.

She sat down close to him and leaned so only he could hear. "A man accosted me out in the crowd."

He went very still. "Who was he?"

"I don't know, but he called me Marie. He seemed to know me."

Nico rose. "Where did he go?" he asked quickly, looking back the way she'd come.

She shook her head and reached to tug on his sleeve, pulling him back down. "You'll never find him now. He disappeared into the crowd." She licked her dry lips. "He…he gave me a warning."

Nico dropped back down close to her. "What sort of warning?"

She closed her eyes for a few seconds. She hated doing this. For one thing, it put her into a category that wasn't flattering. And she was very much afraid she might just belong there.

Taking a deep breath, she raised her chin and went on. "He said someone named Umberto would make things ugly for me if I didn't contact him very soon."

"Umberto?"

"That's the name he said."

"And you don't know…?"

"No." She shook her head, feeling tragic. "I don't remember that name at all."

He frowned, thinking for a moment. "Don't go out on your own again," he warned her. "Stay near security. And tell me right away if you see him in the crowd."

She nodded. The joy in the day was gone and a sick feeling lay at the pit of her stomach. There were so many questions. Why was she running? What if she was part of some sort of smuggling ring? What if she belonged to a den of thieves, a Mafia family, a gang of grifters? Why did she have coded papers in her clothes? Why did hard-eyed men with rough faces seem to know her?

She did want to find out about her own life. But she was very much afraid that once she knew the truth, once they all knew the truth, she was never going to see Nico again.

She thought about that during the ride back home in the dark that evening. Staring out into the black night, her future was beginning to shape itself from the mist and that future was going to have nothing in common with this royal family. Evidence seemed clear. One way or another, she was involved with some vulgar people. And there was no way she was going to do anything that might tarnish the reputation of this royal family and this royal prince. She felt as though she was back at the beginning again, as she'd been the first night she'd arrived at the palace. She had to get away.

She was up early the next morning, but Nico was up even earlier. By the time she came down to the breakfast room, he was there with a list of all the Umbertos in the kingdom.

"I'm not sure how complete it is," he admitted, handing it to her. "This just goes to prove how important it is to get a modern computer network up and running in this country. Our data banks are so far behind the rest of Europe. They practically had to go out with questionnaires to get this much."

She glanced down the page, pretty sure it wasn't going to help much. Then she looked at Nico sitting nursing a cup of coffee. She loved the way his dark hair fell over his forehead, the way his blue eyes considered something seriously before the flicker of amusement came back into his gaze. If only…

"I have to tell you something," she said quietly. "I think I'm beginning to get my memory back."

His gaze sharpened. "Tell me," he said simply.

"Well, it's not as if I'm getting any sudden revelations or anything like that," she said quickly. "It's more like—I begin to realize that more and more of my background is filling in. Think of one of those paint-by-number canvases where the images come in as you fill in the colors. My canvas is beginning to make sense to me. I'm remembering a childhood that I didn't have a couple of days ago. It's all starting to come back to me." She wrinkled her nose in a sort of smile. "I think."

"You think." He smiled into her eyes. "Let me know everything, okay?"

"Okay." She loved his smile, loved feeling warmed by it. "Let's just hope it's really *my* past, and not someone else's," she added.

He laughed. Rising, he stopped beside her. Her heart began to beat in a crazy pattern in her chest, but all he did was touch her shoulder and then move on, getting ready for his day. She closed her eyes as he left the room. Oh yes, she was going to miss this.

Carla came down for breakfast and they had some fun going over the previous day's events, especially the visit from Jans Hunsinger, which seemed to have left Carla head over heels in infatuation. Marisa had some concerns about that. Something about the young man hadn't sat right with her.

She was coming back from a stroll in the forest around noon when Nico hailed her from the terrace.

"I've got some news for you from Intelligence," he said when she got close enough. "From markings on that cookbook they were able to pinpoint the language of those symbols."

"No kidding." She joined him and they both sat at a little round table with a sweeping view of the palace grounds. "What language is it?"

"It seems to belong to a tiny area in the hill country north of Bennire. It's very remote there and a tribe of ancients set up a protected enclave around a monks' castle where they developed their own language and way of writing. This was all in the thirteenth century."

She frowned. "Well, that's very interesting, but what does it have to do with me?"

He shrugged. "Who knows? This language is so obscure there really isn't much about it in the field. They've sent for an expert who is coming by the end of the week. In the meantime, one thing they can say for sure is that part of the writings on your papers are recipes."

"Recipes?" She gaped at him. "How could recipes be so important I would hide them in the lining of a skirt?"

"That is still a mystery. But it does fit with your obvious talent as a cook, doesn't it?"

She sighed, head in her hands as she leaned on the table.

"So I guess the news is that I'm not a spy after all," she said, feeling a bit sorry to see that go. "It looks like I might be some sort of cook." She looked at him sideways. "I don't know that it's any better that way." What she knew for sure was the fact that cooks and princes did not mix. Not romantically, at any rate.

"Hey, there's nothing better than a sexy cook."

She gave him a look. "How would you know? How many cooks have you dallied with in your time?"

"Hundreds." His eyes warmed her. "But none as sexy as you."

She laughed. "Who else in the world would

call a pregnant woman sexy?" she asked, hoping her eyes weren't telegraphing the full affection she was feeling.

"Anyone who took a good look at you."

He wanted to kiss her. The impulse was clear in his eyes. One touch and she would melt. She was so in love with this man. Rising abruptly, she mumbled an excuse, and ran to her room, her heart beating wildly. She wasn't going to be able to resist her feelings much longer. She had to get out of here. She had to do it soon.

Nico sank into a deep chair in the library and stared at a shelf full of books, going into full brooding mode. He didn't want to live without her. That realization was growing stronger and stronger inside him. She was the morning sunlight, the cool caress of moonlight in the evening. He wanted to breathe the air around her. He wanted to see her face when he woke up, feel her body when he lay in bed, hear her soft voice in his ear every day. He needed her. So what was he going to do about it?

Marry her. That was the only way for a man like him. He had to marry her. Just making that decision, just letting himself view it as a possibility, lightened his spirits immensely. He would marry her. They would make a family together.

That was the way it had to be. He had to stay. He had to be a part of the restoration. His whole life was devoted to it. But he had to do it with Marisa by his side. Yes. His mind was made up.

Now, how was he going to convince her of it?

CHAPTER TEN

THE situation seemed to be perfectly timed. Carla and Aunt Julia were on an overnight visit to the Duke of Gevetia's summer estate. The Belgrade cousins, Jan and Jols were at the theater. Prince Nico was at a late meeting at Parliament. Even Chauncy had taken some rare time off. Marisa was going to take this opportunity to make her escape at last.

She had to wear one of Nadia's outfits because she had no choice, but she wasn't packing anything to take along. She agonized over a note to Nico, finally settling on a simple thank you with regrets.

And then she had one thing left to do. She had to get her coded papers back. After all, she'd gone through a lot because of them. They must be important to her real life. She didn't think she ought to try to get away without them.

That meant she had to get into the prince's suite and hope the papers were there. She made sure there was no one to see her, then raced up the stairs and tried the door to his room. It opened without any problem, and she was inside, and suddenly out of breath. She stopped, trying to calm herself. It wasn't that she had run so hard coming up the stairs. It was more because she was scared to death. In some ways, that was a relief. Maybe she wasn't such a bad person after all if she couldn't break into someone's room without feeling awful about it.

She got her breathing under control and opened the tall closet, pulling open the flat drawer. There they were. She was just reaching for them when the door to the room opened and Nico walked in.

She screamed—more evidence that she wasn't used to doing things like this. But Nico nearly jumped out of his skin, then stood staring at her as though she might be a ghost.

"What are you doing here?" he demanded.

She knew what this looked like. After all, he'd thought she was a spy from the beginning. She had a perfectly good explanation—sort of—but she was so unsettled, she couldn't get it out, and instead stood there saying, "I—I—I" over and over again and waving the papers at him.

"You wanted to look at the papers?" he asked skeptically, his face impassive, his eyes cold as steel. "Why didn't you just ask?"

Why not indeed? "Uh…" She licked her lips. "Oh Nico, you've got me so shook up I can't even think straight," she managed at last. "You scared me to death coming in like that. I—I thought you were at Parliament."

The corners of his mouth tweaked and his face began to soften a bit. Obviously, she'd stumbled on to exactly the right tone to lower his suspicions.

"They were all yelling at each other and getting nowhere. I decided to come home and try to get some sleep."

"And I'm in your way." She smiled but knew it must look ghastly. That was certainly the way it felt. "Look, do you mind if I just take these papers back to my room so I can look them over? I—I had some thoughts."

"Sure. Why not?"

He pulled off his tie and draped it across the back of a chair, then began working on the buttons of his shirt. She tried to start gathering up the papers, but somehow she couldn't stop watching him undress.

"You don't have to go right away, do you?" he asked her softly.

She swallowed hard but didn't answer. Not with words, anyway. Her eyes, however, were another story. They were so dark, so huge, so warm, he felt as though he could lose himself in them. There was such sadness there, and yet, there was something so full of a sensual promise, he couldn't turn away.

She knew exactly what she was doing and she knew she shouldn't be. But this was the last time she would ever see him, and it broke her heart. So when he started toward her, she didn't move away or do anything at all to resist or deter him.

Instead, she turned into his arms and raised her face for his kiss.

His lips touched hers, then his tongue traced their edges and she moaned, opening her mouth to invite him inside. He filled her with his heat, gathering her up in his arms and pulling her close. She clung to him, luxuriating in his kiss, pressing her breasts against him, feeling the evidence of how much he wanted her and letting the growing excitement in her own body run uncontrolled.

He wanted her and she wanted him and she couldn't think of anything else. He was all she needed. He tasted dark and rich and hot and she wanted all of him with an urgency she couldn't hide.

"Marisa," he whispered close to her ear. "Are you sure?"

She turned her head and caught his mouth with hers in answer, arching her body against him, lifting her arms to encircle his neck and showing him in every way she could how much she needed him. He kissed the tender spot at her ear, kissed his way down her neck, kissed the pulse at the base of her throat, then reached up to tug down the zipper of her top, exposing the swell of her breasts to more kisses.

Her hands slid beneath his shirt and pushed it away from his hot flesh. He felt like liquid gold beneath her touch. She stroked his chest, his back, his sides, her hands sliding all the way down to where his slacks began. She couldn't stop, and when he shuddered under her touch, she felt a power she'd never known she could have.

Somehow they had landed on the bed. Somehow, their limbs were entwined and their bodies were trembling with anticipation. Marisa had never felt so alive. She'd never felt so in love. She'd never felt so ready to make love.

But a sudden sound, like an explosion, ripped through the house. They both stopped, alert and listening. There was shouting and more banging. Something was going on.

Nico rolled away from her, rose from the bed and went to the door. Opening it, he listened for a moment, then groaned.

"Oh my God. It's Dane."

Nico's brother and the future King of Carnethia could be heard storming through the open areas downstairs like a menacing tornado. There was yelling, there were people scurrying.

"Stay here," Nico advised grimly, putting his shirt on. "I'll go see what the problem is."

Marisa blinked, steadying herself. How could she stay here when all hell seemed to be breaking loose downstairs? Something told her whatever the problem was, it was going to touch her life. She couldn't just wait here and wonder. Pulling her clothing to rights and fluffing her hair, she looked back at the bed with regret, then carefully followed him down the stairs and into the foyer where his brother was holding forth.

Dane was just as handsome as his two brothers, but thicker and fiercer. He'd brought a couple of men with him, and Chauncy had appeared, but Dane was the center of the disturbance. He was waving a newspaper around and speaking emphatically, but she still hadn't caught what he was so upset about. And then he saw her.

"You!" he said, turning to face her, his eyes steely, his tone pure sarcasm. "You're the one. I hear you're carrying my baby."

Her mouth dropped and she turned to look at Nico.

"Don't bully her," Nico said, quickly coming between them protectively. "It's not her fault."

Dane slapped the newspaper he held. "Then tell me, Nico, whose fault is it? I get up this morning and the papers are full of it. Look at this headline— Mother of Future King Hidden in Palace."

He glared at Marisa. "That's you, I take it." He pulled another paper out of a briefcase. "And this one: Found: The Missing Royal Heir. Or how about, Dane's Babe Uncovered."

Nico shook his head, appalled. "Those are just crazy."

"Of course they are. But these people don't care about that. They get a hint of scandal and they run with it." Dane shook his head, looking fierce. "I spend half my time trying to convince you all how detrimental it would be if you get written up in the tabloids, and the next thing I know, out of the blue, *I'm* written about." He waved the papers at Nico again. "I want to know how this happened."

Nico took a paper from him and read the headline for himself. Swearing, he dropped it again. "This was today in Paris? Our local rags will have picked it up by tomorrow, no doubt about it."

"And wait until you read the body of the article. They know things about us I didn't know *we* knew. Now you tell me. How did they get these details?"

Nico stared at him without saying a word. Marisa's heart began to race and her head began to pound.

"I'll tell you how," the crown prince said. "We have only one new element among us."

Everyone turned and stared at Marisa. Shock flashed through her like an electric charge.

"You're blaming me?" she asked in horror. "I didn't have a thing to do with it. I wouldn't even know how to contact this sort of journalist."

Dane gave her a scathing look. "You don't have to worry about that. They'll contact you if they get the idea you might be willing to spill your guts for them. A little information can yield a lot of cash."

"Well, there you go," she said, working hard to hold back any sign of panic. "You can ask Prince Nico. I don't have any money. Case closed."

"No outside bank accounts?" Dane asked, arching a rugged eyebrow.

"Listen, I don't even have a cell phone to use to call the papers with. You may not know this, but I've had amnesia for the last week or so and…"

Dane waved a hand dismissively. "I know all about it—how Nico found you trying to jump off a bridge and all. My family has graciously taken you in while you are recovering, and this is how you repay us."

She felt sick, dizzy, breathless. Her head ached so badly she could hardly stand it. That made it hard to think, hard to figure out a way to defend herself. Prince Dane really seemed to believe that she had done this thing. She looked at Nico. His eyes were unreadable. Her heart sank. He believed it too.

"I didn't do it," she said hoarsely. She put a hand on her rounded belly. "Why would I want anyone to believe this is your child?"

Dane shrugged. "The usual reason, I suppose. Money."

She shook her head, feeling faint.

"These papers are obsessed with our story. They seem to want to write anything about our family, especially if it has to do with the succession." Suddenly, his anger dulling, he mainly looked tired. "The rumor is that the war wounds I sustained or the malaria I had for awhile, or both, have rendered me unable to have children. That I'm sterile."

Without thinking, Marisa asked the unthinkable. "Are you?"

Most in the room gasped, and she winced, wishing she could recall the question, but her head ached so, she hardly knew what she was doing.

Dane looked at her as though she was so outrageous, it was almost amusing. "You'd like to know, wouldn't you? I suppose there would be a nice bonus for that information." He shook his head in disbelief. "Well, I'm not going to talk about that. The people may think they have a right to know everything about me but there are some things I will keep to myself for the moment."

Going into a more philosophical mood, he began to pace the carpet. "Though when you come right down to it, I can hardly blame our people for being concerned. The fact is, after all this war and uncertainty, they want an heir in the pipeline. They want to see a solid line of succession." He stopped before Marisa and looked her over in an assessing way. "So you are Marisa."

She found herself curtsying and her cheeks reddened.

"Yes, I've heard all about you," he said. "Chauncy keeps me informed."

"Chauncy's a snitch?" Nico said, his voice sharp with irony as he looked around to see the butler slinking out of the room.

"Forget it, Nico," Dane responded. "He's known me longer than he's known you. And loves me better, I daresay."

"No doubt."

The two brothers faced each other warily. Marisa could see there was respect between them, but a measure of resentment as well.

"We need to talk," Dane said wearily.

Nico nodded. "Why don't you go on up to your room?" he said quietly to Marisa. "I've got to hash this out with Dane. I'll see you in the morning."

She nodded, then looked into his eyes, wanting to see something that would give her reason to hope. There was no warmth there, and she cringed inside. He believed she was a crook. And why shouldn't he? Every time he turned around, something pointed in that direction, culminating in him finding her rummaging around in his room.

Blinking back tears, she turned and walked sedately to the stairs, even though she wanted to run. She'd never felt so wrongly accused, and there wasn't a thing she could do to prove her innocence.

But hey—it was her own fault. What had she expected? You couldn't play around with royalty and not expect to get burned.

Once in her room, she didn't waste any time. She was ready to go, wasn't she? Why wait around? If only her head would stop pounding. There was the matter of the papers she'd gone to Nico's room for. She still didn't have them. But there was no way to remedy that now. She had to go without them.

Looking out the front, she saw where the guards were. She knew their routine by now and knew she would have to wait a few minutes before she would have the window of opportunity through which she could slip out.

Glancing down, she saw the simple note she'd written to Nico earlier that evening. Suddenly, she had more to say. Much more. But she had the time. Clearing a place at the vanity table, she sat down, pen in hand, and began to write.

Dane and Nico were squaring off warily as Marisa left for her room. Dane dismissed the others so they could be alone, and once they were, he raised an eyebrow. "Are you and she…?"

"Never mind," Nico responded impatiently. "I

can see that you have a plan. Just what is it you want to do to remedy this situation?"

"That's why I came to you," Dane said, running a hand through his thick hair. "You're the idea guy." He swore softly, shaking his head. "Women. Nothing but trouble."

Nico frowned. Something about Dane saying that put his back up, big-time. He thought first of Marisa, and then his mind went back to Andrea charging into danger, risking everything for the cause—the return of the Montenevada family to the throne, the vanquishing of the hateful Acredonnas who had plundered the country and made life miserable for millions. That was what Andrea had given her life for. And what now? Had it all been worth it?

"What did we do this for, Dane?" he asked his brother, a thread of tense emotion in his voice. "In some ways, the country is in worse shape than when we began. Have you seen the statistics, the crime in the streets, the profiteering, the graft? Why aren't we doing anything to stem this filthy tide of corruption?"

"Nico, we are doing something. We have plans…"

"Plans, but no action."

Dane stared at him for a moment, realizing these were more than normal complaints. "Nico," he said at last, "I know you still mourn for Andrea. We all do. But she died doing what she had to do. She wouldn't have had it any other way. She was a born warrior."

"She fought for a better country, not…" He shook his head.

"These things take time."

Nico moved impatiently. "Time you don't seem to have to give them. You're out of the country at these international conferences constantly. When is the hard work going to get done here at home?"

"I have to deal with the international alliances before I can turn my full attention to the local problems."

"That's just wrong, Dane. Our people need you to tend to their needs first and foremost. Let the international world go away for awhile."

"Nico, don't you understand?" Dane responded irritably. "Without international ties, we're alone and defenseless in a dangerous world. Right now we're like a newborn baby. We need help to stay alive. Believe me, there are plenty of bigger powers who would love to snap us up if they saw a hint of weakness on our borders." He scowled. "These tabloid stories help promote weakness."

Nico nodded. He agreed with Dane as far as it went. Still… "So what do you want to do about it?"

Dane's head rose and he met his brother's troubled gaze. "The first thing we have to do is remove that woman from the premises. Put her somewhere out of the public eye, where the press can forget about her—and she can forget about us."

"Sorry," Nico said firmly, returning his brother's gaze with implacable resistance. "We're not going to do that."

Dane's face hardened. "We have to do it. It's the only way." He gestured in the direction Marisa had gone. "She's a traitor. I want her out of here."

Nico stood toe to toe with his older brother. "If she goes, so do I."

Dane frowned, shaking his head as though he couldn't believe what he was hearing. "What are you talking about?"

"It's not all about you, Dane. You may be just a few weeks short of becoming king, but that doesn't make you the most important person on earth. Or even in this country. And right now, as far as I'm concerned, Marisa's feelings are more important than you getting your face out of the tabloids." He shook his head. "She didn't do it. And I won't allow you to persecute her for something that's not her fault."

"Well, if she didn't do it, who did?"

"I don't know. But that's our problem, not hers." His eyes narrowed as he faced the future king. "You can have her expelled from the palace. You're the boss. But if she goes, I go."

Dane stared at his brother for a moment, then abruptly shifted gears. "Calm down, Nico," he said quietly. "I need you by my side. Don't throw up barriers."

"Maybe I've had it," Nico said, though he was

talking just as quietly as Dane now. "Maybe it's all gone too far and cost too much. Maybe I should just let you run this damn country by yourself." He shook his head. "I don't even know if it's worth running."

"Oh, it's worth it." The crown prince stared at his brother. "Are you in love with her?"

Nico looked up and saw the humanity in Dane's eyes. "Yes," he said simply. "Yes, I am."

Dane nodded. He took a long, deep breath before he spoke again. "Okay, then. I remember how you were with Andrea. I'll trust your instincts on this, too. I just hope you're right."

Nico's shoulders sagged and all the tension seemed to seep out of him. He took a deep breath of his own and reached out to hug Dane with more awkward affection than grace.

"Thanks," he said, his emotion coloring his voice. "You always were a good guy once you calmed down."

Dane hugged him back roughly. "Hey, it's always been you and me. And it always will be."

CHAPTER ELEVEN

IT wasn't hard to escape from the palace. Marisa had known it wouldn't be. Everything was centered around keeping people out, not locking people in. In no time at all, she was walking quickly down the dark and lonely street. She wasn't as clueless as she'd been the other night. She had a plan this time. She knew where she wanted to go and what she wanted to do.

But she hadn't gone more than two blocks before she knew she wasn't going to be allowed to do things her way. A man was suddenly walking beside her, sliding an arm through hers and sticking something that felt very much like the barrel of a gun in her ribs.

"So there you are, Marie," the cold masculine voice ground out in her ear. "Umberto will be happy to have you home again. He's got plans for you."

She didn't have to turn to know it was the same man who'd accosted her at the races. Closing her eyes, she sighed with resignation.

"It's Tom Verner, isn't it?" she said. "I remember now."

Prince Nico was up early the next morning. He had some work to go over before breakfast, so he was available to take an early phone call from his security staff.

"Good morning, Your Highness. We've got a painter here who claims he's found a suitcase we've been searching for. He was assigned to paint the underside of the Gonglia Bridge and there it was, stuck up under the pilings where it couldn't be seen…"

"I'll be right there," Nico said. He glanced toward the stairway that led to Marisa's room, wondering if he should wake her and take her along, but decided against it. There was plenty of time for her to see the bag later. They had all day.

It certainly looked as if it could be hers. He had it brought into the library and put on the library table, but he didn't want to open it without her. He was surprised she wasn't down yet. She usually showed up before anyone else. He hesitated. He had to remember she was carrying a baby and might need more sleep. He didn't want to disturb her. He waited another half hour, then threw caution to the winds and ran up the stairs and knocked on her door.

When she didn't respond, he knew right away that she was gone. Throwing open the door, he charged inside and cursed loudly. The bed hadn't been slept in. Why hadn't he realized she would finally make good on her need to go? And now, how was he going to find her again?

Just as he turned to leave the room, his eye caught the note on the vanity. He stopped, picked it up, then sank into a chair while he read it.

My dearest Prince Nico,
I didn't tell the tabloids anything. I'm so sorry you think I did.

I've got to go. I'm starting to remember more and more and I think I know why I ran, why I ended up where you found me that night. And why I must go back.

I came to this city hoping to find refuge with a wealthy and influential uncle I hadn't seen for years. I never did contact him. I don't even know if he still lives here in town. I know I was running because of a man named Umberto. He's the father of my baby. He's a criminal. He conned me into a relationship and some financial deals. I know I never married him.

My family has made chocolate for over two hundred years. We make the best gourmet chocolate in this part of Europe. Umberto came to work for me when my father joined the rebel army and disappeared into the mountains. He was charming and smart and handsome. It was amazing how he took to chocolate work. I'd never seen anyone take to it the way he did, so quickly, so expertly. He bowled me over. I'd never known a man, other than my father, who loved it the way I did. Of course, it was all a lie. I found out later when the truth came out that he'd been a chocolatier as long as I had—from birth, and he'd showed up on my doorstep when he did in order to steal my family's recipes. By the time I realized all this, I was pregnant and he had swindled me out of my family's company.

I have to go back and face him and somehow get my company back. And that is the trajectory of my future life—so different from yours.

Goodbye, sweet prince. Thank you so much for all you and your family have done for me. Tell Carla I love her. May your family's reign in this country be long and fruitful. I'll be pulling for you all the way.

Nico stared at the page. It took a few minutes to fully digest all that she'd said. But the reality of her leaving hadn't changed. And he still didn't know her real name, though the man at the track had called her Marie. But where to begin to go to find her. Stuffing the paper into his pocket, he went back downstairs and into the library. Taking out a screwdriver, he began to work on the lock on the suitcase. In a moment he had it open, and in among the various clothing and cosmetics he found what they had been looking for all this time—the key to the code. The papers were the recipes, the key would let someone read them. Finally.

But a more important item was missing. Nowhere did he find a name or an address. He reached for the telephone. Intelligence was going to have to try again to come to the rescue.

An hour later, he was sitting at a conference table working madly at a computer, surrounded by intelligence officers and his brother, Dane. Stacks of paper littered the room, lists of food companies, lists of merchandisers, lists of chocolate makers and chocolate sellers. And everybody seemed to be talking at once.

"Quiet!" Dane thundered at last, running his hands through his thick auburn hair until it stood up like a stand of trees on his head. "I can't hear myself think."

"You're not supposed to be thinking," Nico retorted. "You're supposed to be searching. Come on. We don't have any time."

Dane turned and looked at him in disgust. "Did it ever occur to you that just because the woman thinks her company was the best chocolatier in the country doesn't mean it was actually true?"

"It's true," Nico said calmly. "Keep looking."

Dane frowned at him. "Maybe you should take this as a sign," he said more quietly, meant just for his brother. "Maybe you should let her go. Maybe this was just not meant to be."

The words chilled Nico. A small part of him was saying the same thing. But he wasn't buying it. He was going to find her. He was going to find her and ask her to marry him. And if she said no, he was going to sling her over his shoulder and bring her back here and ply her with food and drink and lots of love until she said yes. She had to marry him. Had to.

"Hey," one of the intelligence officers cried out. "What about this one? Geers chocolates. DuBonnet Chocolatier. It's a really old establishment set in a little town in the Bristol Mountains. They list the owner as Charles DuBonnet."

"Does he have a wife?" Nico asked, his heart beginning to pound in dread of what he might hear.

"Yes."

"What's her name?"

"Uh…wait, I saw it here somewhere."

Nico held his breath. If she turned out to be married after all this…

"Here it is. Her name is Grace."

"Oh." He let the breath out in relief.

"But there seems to be a daughter who has taken over just recently."

"Her name?"

"Marie. Marie DuBonnet."

Nico closed his eyes. That had to be it.

"Chauncy, have them bring the car around," he called, bolting out of his chair. "I'm going to the Bristol Mountains."

* * *

Marisa sat across the table from Umberto. Her memory had been almost completely restored by now. Her real name was Marie DuBonnet, owner and operator of DuBonnet Chocolatier. And she had stupidly allowed this man to take over her company and her life.

She watched as he downed another glass of her vintage wine. Shaking her head, she wondered how she ever could have found him attractive. He was mean and vicious and she had the new bruises to prove it. All she could think of was the contrast to Nico with his intellect and integrity. In her mind the prince had taken on the attributes of the perfect hero. Umberto—not so much.

"Where are the recipes?" he demanded, looking belligerent.

"I told you, I don't have them." She felt calm, serene, sure of herself. That was different and she rather liked it.

"What are you talking about?" he growled at her. "You took them when you left here."

"They're gone. You can search me all you want. They are gone." What luck that she hadn't been able to secrete them out after all. "You have the translations I made for you. And that's all you're going to get."

"Those translations are no good." He glared at her and then spat. "They're not the same as the originals. They don't come out right and you know it."

She had to smile, because she did know it. That was why she'd written them that way. He had no right to her ancient family recipes and she was going to make sure he never got his hands on them.

If only she'd understood what he wanted from the beginning. But she hadn't known his background then. His family, the Geers, had run a small chocolate company in another region of the country that was almost as old as her family's. Their quality was never top tier and the family had always seemed to operate at the fringe of what was legal and ethical. The DuBonnets had never paid much attention to them. It might have been better if they had, then they might have noticed how much the Geers hated them. For generations, the Geers had built up feelings of being oppressed by Marisa's family operation. Umberto was raised with that. The whole focus of his life was to find a way to get back at the hated DuBonnets and steal the wealth his family felt they'd been cheated out of.

Now here the two of them sat in the outer office of her family company. Plaques and commendations covered the walls and displays of old-fashioned chocolate-making equipment were set out behind glass and on the open counters. Back through the swinging doors, workers who knew and loved her were busy making some of the best chocolate in Europe. But not the specialty items, the twisted bird's nest mocha, the ballerina lace scrollwork, the dark Brazilian corea. They hadn't been able to make those for some time now. They didn't have the recipes.

"I'm not afraid of you anymore, Umberto," she told him, shooting daggers with her eyes. "You can't do anything to hurt me and my chocolate company. You can make faux

DuBonnet chocolates all day long. Everyone will know they're fakes. It won't work. You should just go back to your own company and try to work on that quality issue you people seem to have."

She braced herself, ready for him to hit her again. Surprisingly, he held off. Leaning close, he told her through clenched teeth, "I am going to make you sorry, Marie. I am going to take you down to the cellar where no one can see what I do to you. I'll keep you down there as long as it takes. But you are going to give me those damn recipes."

"Never," she said firmly, eyes clear.

He almost hit her then. Holding himself back, he was breathing hard. "I've got my boys, Tom and Willie, to help me. I think we can handle you between us."

Even that didn't frighten her. Funny how she now had the strength to stand up to him on her own. She didn't need the help of her uncle or anyone else. She could tell him straight to his face what she thought.

"I realize something now," she told him, just for his information. "Even if you got hold of the old recipes, it wouldn't help you. Your chocolate will never be the same as ours. Because you don't have the love of chocolate we have always had. You love revenge, not chocolate." She smiled. "I reject you, Umberto. I reject everything about you. I won't be a part of you in any way."

He stared at her in impotent rage. "So you think because you've become the prince's concubine you'll be protected?" he sneered.

That little dart hit its mark, she had to admit, but she tried not to show it. He turned, reaching for the wine bottle. He was still talking, listing all the things he was going to do to her and the way he was going to make her pay if she didn't hand over the real recipes to him. She knew very well he was planning to make her pay even if she did as he demanded.

It was lucky he had no interest in the child, though he knew about her pregnancy. Because of that, he didn't realize how much he could hurt her through her baby. It hadn't occurred to him yet. But that didn't mean it never would. She had to do something but she had a strange calmness about her. She knew she was going to handle this. She had to.

She looked at the display tools sitting on the open counter, the grinders and the sifters and the mallets. The largest mallet was almost within reach and she stared at it, thinking of all the hard chocolate that had been crushed into powder by that mallet over the years. She rather hated to defile it, but there wasn't much choice. Rising smoothly, quietly, she picked it up, took a deep breath, gritted her teeth and swung hard at his head, then watched as he grunted and dropped to the ground. He was out like a light.

"With a swing like that, you should consider trying out for the New York Yankees."

She spun on her heel and found Nico standing in the doorway. Her heart leaped up. "Oh, Nico!" she cried, hurling herself into his arms. "You found me!"

He smiled down at her, holding on as though

he knew just how precious she was. "Were you lost?" he teased softly.

"Oh, yes!"

"Well, you left enough bread crumbs. I could hardly have missed the trail."

She turned her tearstained face up and he dropped a kiss on her lips, then put her to the side so that he could walk over and nudge Umberto's body with his foot.

"Looks like he's still out. Too bad. I would have paid good money to see you swing that mallet at him again." He shook his head in raw admiration, then pulled out a cell phone.

"What are you doing?" Marisa asked him.

"Calling the police. We need to get him locked up before he comes to. I have a feeling he's going to be in a very bad mood."

Marisa shook her head. Everything was happening pretty fast, and she was trying to keep up. "He has two henchmen who are…"

"Yes, I know. I've got a couple of men with me. We ran into them outside. They've been taken care of as well."

"Oh."

She watched him talk into the phone and her love for him almost choked her. This was all so surreal. One minute she'd been fighting for her life and the next, here was the prince to take care of everything. But that meant they were back to the basic question—just what was he doing here?

"I still don't understand how you found me," she said and he closed his phone.

"Your suitcase showed up. The man who mugged you threw it over the side of the bridge, but it seems it never actually fell. It got caught up in the scaffolding under the bridge in such a way that it wasn't visible from the bridge or the ground. It wasn't until a painter was climbing under the rafters that he saw it."

"So you opened it?"

"I had to. Once I'd read your letter, I knew I had to find you. It was my only lead."

She nodded. "So you saw the key to the code."

"Yes. From there it just took time to figure out which chocolate company was yours."

She shook her head. "I'm so glad you're such a good detective," she noted. "I left the palace around midnight and Tom Verner, one of Umberto's men, grabbed me right away. In fact, he was the one who mugged me the other night. And I'm sure he was the one I saw watching the palace that time."

Prince Nico was frowning. "Why would he mug you?"

"To get the recipes. He wore a bandana over his face, but I knew it was him." She made a face. "Until I didn't know it anymore. For over a week."

"But your mind is clear now."

"Oh yes. Totally." Quickly, she explained Umberto's background, how he'd hoped to steal her company secrets and ended up taking control of DuBonnet Chocolatier to such a degree she had to go for help. "He worked with me for months, learning all our methods. But once I began to realize he didn't deserve to know our secrets, he'd already made me sign papers that gave him part ownership. So I sewed the coded recipes in my skirt and destroyed the other copies. I gave him false copies instead. When he realized it, he tried to force me to give him the real ones and that's when I ran. I was hoping to find my uncle and get his protection and help, getting control of my company again that way. But Tom followed me. He thought he would find the recipes in my suitcase or my purse, so he knocked me down and threw them over the side of the bridge, hoping to pick them up later downstream. Only the suitcase didn't show up. So he kept following me until I disappeared into the palace. He couldn't follow me in, so he waited for his chance."

"Thank God I found you when I did."

"Yes." She smiled at him, loving everything about him.

"But explain these recipes to me. What makes them so special?"

"The oldest ones aren't even chocolate. They're various methods of mixing ingredients with sugar to form the base of our candies. These methods were developed in that little monastery in the mountains where that strange code language was used. One of my ancestors was given sanctuary in that monastery in the thirteenth century. He came away with the recipes and started making sweets. Later, when chocolate came from the New World, the DuBonnets incorporated those recipes in a special way informed by the old ones. And that is why we have such unique taste and texture."

"And now you've ended up saving your recipes after all."

"Yes. Thanks to you." She sighed. "You gave me the refuge I needed to get the distance to understand that I had options. I didn't have to be a victim." She sneaked a glance his way. "So I'm not a spy. And I'm not an archeology student. But I am a cook of sorts."

More than an ordinary cook, still, less than royal—or anywhere near that. She knew the gulf between them was still huge, and it included his suspicions about her having leaked family information to the press. But he'd come to the rescue at just the right time and she'd needed him— more for emotional support than anything else, still, she had never been so glad to see anyone in her life.

The police had arrived and she and Nico moved outside so that they could watch the removal from a distance. The air was full of the scent of fruit trees blooming. It was spring. Time for renewal. They stood back and looked at her company and he put his arm around her shoulders, pulling her close.

"So this is your chocolate factory," he said, looking over the Tudor-style cottage that was its main office. "Looks like something out of a storybook. I expect to see the Seven Dwarves coming out of the doors and windows singing 'Hi Ho' at any moment."

She smiled, pleased with his tone. "Do you like it? It's really a wonderful place."

"I can see that."

She frowned. "Of course, Umberto is part owner."

"Don't worry, we've got lawyers to untangle that sort of problem."

She looked up, searching his face. "Nico, why did you come after me?"

He looked down into hers. "I wanted to make sure you were okay."

She tried to smile but suddenly there was a lump in her throat. "Was that all?" she asked, disappointed and trying to hold it back.

His brow furled thoughtfully. "No, there was one other thing."

"Yes?"

He looked down as though he could drown in her eyes. "I just wanted to know if you..."

The siren on the police car went off, making them both jump.

"Oh!" she cried.

He held her closer as the vehicles drove off.

"What was it you were wondering about me?" she asked, prompting him to get back on track.

"Oh, nothing much," he said casually, pushing her hair back so he could look into her pretty face. "I just was wondering if you'd like to get married. That's all."

"Get married?" She frowned. What on earth was he talking about?

"Yes."

She shook her head, completely perplexed. "Get married to whom?"

He looked around as though expecting someone else. "How about me?" he suggested. "I'm the one who loves you."

She blinked at him, waiting for the catch. But there was a smile growing in his eyes. "Are you kidding?" she asked at last. "You don't mean…"

"Marisa, are you going to make me go down on one knee?" he asked lightly.

"Nico, don't tease me!"

"I'm not. I love you. Maybe you hadn't noticed. Here, I'll show you."

He kissed her with passion and intensity and she gasped for breath when he was finished.

"You still haven't said yes," he demanded.

"But…"

"You hesitate. Do you realize what you're doing to my ego? Listen, there are plenty of benefits to marrying a prince."

Her smile was tremulous and tears filled her eyes. "I don't know," she said, trying to join in the spirit of the jest. "All those boring state dinners."

"We can find ways to make them interesting. We could invite chocolate makers from all over the world. You could be queen of chocolate."

She laughed. Was everything really going to be all right? It was hard to get her mind around that. There had to be a catch.

"But does Dane still suspect me of leaking family information?"

"No, not at all." He waved her worries away as though she shouldn't have given that a second thought.

"But *you* did. At least at first."

"Never. Not for a moment. And I told Dane that right after you left the room."

He was so candid, she believed him totally. She was so relieved.

"And anyway, the mystery is solved. Carla got home before I left this morning and she confessed everything."

"What? Carla?" This news was as shocking to her as everything else that had happened that day.

"Yes. You remember that Jans Hunsinger who hovered around her at the derby?"

"Of course."

"He charmed her and somehow he contacted her and got her to call him secretly. Chatted her up and got all sorts of info out of her. Turns out he's actually a writer for one of those rags."

"Oh no." Marisa gasped. "Poor Carla."

"Don't worry. She'll be okay. She's young and bound to make mistakes." He dropped another kiss on her lips. "She has to learn how to act like a princess. You already seem to be a natural." His mouth twisted in appreciation of the concept. "You're natural royalty. Chocolate royalty."

She laughed. Everything was making her laugh. She'd never been so happy. "You could say that, I suppose."

"I can see the headlines now: 'The chocolate queen deigns to marry a lowly prince of the realm.' I think the tabloids would love it."

"But Dane wouldn't." Her face changed. "Oh! Quick. Give me your hand." She placed his palm right over where the little foot was kicking. "Do you feel that?"

"Hey!" He pulled his hand back, startled. "This

baby does more than talk, doesn't she?" he said, but he put his palm on her belly again and this time he smiled. "Marisa," he said. "That's amazing."

"Isn't it?"

Emotion choked him suddenly, and he thought of Andrea and the baby that should have reached this stage but never had. Marisa was so different from his first love. And yet, there were some very important similarities—strength, beauty, wonderful humor and just plain goodness. She was perfect. Even Andrea would approve.

"Nico, tell me honestly," Marisa was saying, searching his eyes. "What do you think about children?"

He shrugged. "She'll be the first. More to come."

Marisa's worry showed in her face. "Promise me that you won't love her any less than the others who come later."

He held her in the circle of his arms. "How could I? She's a part of you." He dropped a kiss on her neck, then another. "In fact, she'll always be first in my heart. After all, if she hadn't existed, we might never have met."

She sighed, running on pure happiness. "And all because of chocolate," she noted happily. "Want to go in and try some?"

He smiled. "I thought you'd never ask."

But he kissed her first, just because he could.

EPILOGUE

"SHHH." Carla put a finger to her lips and cautioned Marisa. "I can't tell you yet," she whispered. "It's a secret."

A secret. Marisa stared at her soon-to-be-sister-in-law in frustration. Here she was, standing in a cold, damp basement room in her wedding gown, and Carla was telling her she couldn't know where she was going or what would happen once she got there. What sort of wedding was this?

She knew Dane was opposed to her marrying his brother. He'd made that very clear. And Nico had made it just as clear that he would give up his right of succession before he would give up the woman he loved.

"Give it some time," Dane had urged just days

before. "Later this year when this nonsense in the tabloids has died down we can look at a public announcement…if you still feel the way you do now. But we're barely getting our footing with the public. To have you marry a pregnant commoner of no standing will send the chattering classes into a frenzy. We can't afford that in this precarious atmosphere."

"If we wait," Nico had responded firmly, "Marisa's baby will be born out of wedlock. And everyone will assume the baby isn't mine."

Dane had given him a puzzled look. "But…the baby isn't yours."

Nico had smiled. "That's where you're wrong, brother. That baby became mine as soon as I realized how much I loved Marisa. I take full responsibility. Nothing will change that. And our marriage will confirm it."

Dane's anger began to show itself. "You're crazy," he'd said with a fierce frown. "Life doesn't work that way. And as for this insane marriage, I forbid it!"

Nico had set his jaw and turned away. With a

sinking heart, Marisa had assumed that was going to be the final word. Later that evening, he'd told her he was taking a short trip to Paris and would be gone for a few days. Three days later, Carla had appeared in her room with news and very sparkling eyes.

"Come quickly! Nico is back. He's brought you a wedding gown. It's in my room. You're to put it on and then I'm to take you to the dungeon."

"What?"

"Don't worry. It's just the basement and wine cellar. We always call it the dungeon because…" She shrugged with a disarming smile. "Well, just because. Come on. There's no time to lose."

They'd rushed through the preparations. Marisa's heart was beating like a drum. She tried to find out what Carla thought of it all, whether she thought it was wise to go against Dane this way, but Carla refused to discuss it.

"We don't have time to talk," she'd said, slipping into a lovely blue silk number that was a perfect complement to the satin and lace Marisa was sinking into. "Hurry! Here's your veil."

"Oh," Marisa sighed. Beautifully studded with tiny freshwater pearls, it was a lacy fantasy. Once it was installed, looking through it felt like looking into a magical future. Was she really going to marry the man of her dreams? It seemed hard to believe.

"And your flowers."

White orchids with violet centers in a stunning waterfall spray. Looking into the full-length mirror, she gasped. She looked incredible, if she did say so herself.

"Let's go."

And now here they were, waiting in the basement. Marisa looked around at the gloomy walls and shivered, wondering if the place had actually been used as a dungeon after all. Maybe that creepy sense of presence she was feeling was really the ghosts of past unwilling visitors and...

She stopped cold. The ground was shaking. Earthquake? Heart in her throat, she turned to look at Carla who was shaking her head.

"Look," she said, pointing toward the back

wall. Marisa turned. The back wall had split and was rumbling open. A long, wide passage was revealed, flickering torches lining the way. And just inside stood what looked like a golden sleigh set on an electric track.

"Let's go," Carla said, picking up the bride's long white train and nodding toward the sleigh.

"What is this?" Marisa asked as they settled into the plush seats. The doors rumbled shut behind them and the sleigh took off down the track.

"This was the royal family's escape route during the overthrow fifty years ago," Carla explained. "During medieval times it was the secret way out of the palace. During the Reformation, it was the secret passage to the royal family's private chapel. And now…" She smiled at her soon-to-be-sister. "Now it's the secret pathway to your wedding."

Marisa smiled back, but before she had time to ask more questions, the sleigh was slowing. They had arrived at the secret royal chapel, and there was Prince Mychale, looking elegant and debonair in tails, to escort her into the sanctuary.

"Hello, Your Highness," she said as she took his arm and stepped down onto the stone floor.

"Welcome, Marisa," he said, smiling down at her. "I can tell you'll be a wonderful addition to our clan. We're very pleased to have you."

"Thank you," she told him, her tone heartfelt. "I can't tell you how honored I am to be j-j-joining you." She still felt shy and tentative about how unworthy she was and about Crown Prince Dane's disapproval, and that made it difficult for her to talk about it casually.

Mychale had her pause with him at the doorway. An organ inside began to play "The Wedding March." Marisa gulped. This was it. Suddenly the doors were thrown open. For just a moment she was blinded by the light coming from the beautiful, high, stained-glass ceiling, but once her gaze cleared, she saw Prince Nico standing at the end of the aisle, waiting for her.

With a cry of delight she dropped Mychale's arm and ran to her love. He laughed, catching her up in his arms and twirling her for a moment. Then he stopped, setting her down where she belonged, and she noticed the priest who was waiting to perform the service. Her heart was beating so hard, she was sure she was about to faint. Carla came up and took her place beside her. She looked to see if Mychale was standing up with Nico, but he was off to the side, and she frowned, wondering why.

And then she saw why. An imposing figure entered the chapel and came directly toward where they were standing. Her breath stopped in her throat. It was Dane. What was he doing here? Her head snapped around as she looked at Nico, wondering if they should run for it. But Nico was smiling, and as she watched, mouth open in wonder, Dane took the position for the best man.

"Nico?" she whispered loudly.

He gave her a wink and nodded. "Dane's come around," he whispered back.

"Oh!" She smiled at the future king, joy rushing in her veins. "Oh, thank you, Your Majesty," she whispered so loudly, it seemed to ring from wall to wall.

Dane grinned at her. "I'm not a 'majesty' yet," he reminded her. "So I decided to put off trying to run everyone's life around here until I'm legally obligated to do so."

The priest cleared his throat and they all came to attention like naughty schoolchildren. It was time to begin.

Most of the short service left Marisa in a daze. She knew she'd said "I do" and she knew she'd given Nico a ring and received one of her own. And then she distinctly heard, "You may now kiss the bride," and she felt Nico's arms slide around her and his lips press to hers and she sighed, a sound of pure happiness. It was done after all.

He held her tightly, as if he was never going to let her go.

"Marisa," he said softly, close to her ear, "I promise you, as soon as we decide things are stable, we'll have a very huge and very public celebration of our marriage."

She shook her head, looking up at him with tears in her eyes. "Nico, I don't need the public.

I just need you. I'll be your secret bride forever if need be. Just as long as we're together."

And somewhere close by, there was a loud, joyful tolling of a bell.

MILLS & BOON PUBLISH EIGHT LARGE PRINT TITLES A MONTH. THESE ARE THE EIGHT TITLES FOR DECEMBER 2008.

HIRED: THE SHEIKH'S SECRETARY MISTRESS
Lucy Monroe

THE BILLIONAIRE'S BLACKMAILED BRIDE
Jacqueline Baird

THE SICILIAN'S INNOCENT MISTRESS
Carole Mortimer

THE SHEIKH'S DEFIANT BRIDE
Sandra Marton

WANTED: ROYAL WIFE AND MOTHER
Marion Lennox

THE BOSS'S UNCONVENTIONAL ASSISTANT
Jennie Adams

INHERITED: INSTANT FAMILY
Judy Christenberry

THE PRINCE'S SECRET BRIDE
Raye Morgan

MILLS & BOON

Pure reading pleasure™

1108 Rom I

MILLS & BOON PUBLISH EIGHT LARGE PRINT TITLES A MONTH. THESE ARE THE EIGHT TITLES FOR JANUARY 2009.

————————— ✂ —————————

THE DE SANTIS MARRIAGE
Michelle Reid

GREEK TYCOON, WAITRESS WIFE
Julia James

THE ITALIAN BOSS'S
MISTRESS OF REVENGE
Trish Morey

ONE NIGHT WITH HIS VIRGIN MISTRESS
Sara Craven

WEDDING AT WANGAREE VALLEY
Margaret Way

CRAZY ABOUT HER SPANISH BOSS
Rebecca Winters

THE MILLIONAIRE'S PROPOSAL
Trish Wylie

ABBY AND THE PLAYBOY PRINCE
Raye Morgan

MILLS & BOON
Pure reading pleasure™

1208 Rom LP